BRIDE FOR HIRE

by

SERENITY WOODS

Copyright © 2019 Serenity Woods
All rights reserved.
ISBN: 9781690861676

DEDICATION

To Tony & Chris, my Kiwi boys.

CONTENTS

Chapter One 1
Chapter Two 8
Chapter Three 15
Chapter Four 21
Chapter Five 27
Chapter Six 33
Chapter Seven 39
Chapter Eight 47
Chapter Nine 54
Chapter Ten 61
Chapter Eleven 68
Chapter Twelve 75
Chapter Thirteen 82
Chapter Fourteen 90
Chapter Fifteen 96
Chapter Sixteen 102
Chapter Seventeen 108
Chapter Eighteen... 114
Chapter Nineteen 120
Chapter Twenty... 126
Chapter Twenty-One... 133
Chapter Twenty-Two 139
Chapter Twenty-Three 147
Chapter Twenty-Four.. 153
Chapter Twenty-Five 160
Chapter Twenty-Six 167
Chapter Twenty-Seven 173
Newsletter 176
About the Author 177

Chapter One

"I think I'll head off," Cameron Taylor said.

It was late on Saturday evening. His hotel room with the complimentary bathrobe, widescreen TV, and minibar stocked with tiny bottles of Glenlivet beckoned far more than the glam and glitter of the charity ball he'd reluctantly agreed to attend. He had a slight headache, and with Lara no longer available to organize his bow tie for him, he'd done the damn thing up too tight, nearly strangling himself. He should have bought one on a piece of elastic.

"You can't leave me!" His colleague and best friend, Marcus Brant, managed to look aghast even though most of his features were covered by his silver mask. "Promise me you'll stay until midnight."

"I can't." Cameron adjusted his own mask so that it sat on the bridge of his nose more comfortably. A Masquerade Ball. What a stupid idea. Did adults really enjoy this sort of thing? "I'll turn into a pumpkin."

"It was the carriage that turned into a pumpkin," Marcus pointed out. "Not Cinderella. I can tell you don't have young children."

"I got confused," Cameron said. "I thought you were one of the ugly sisters." He ignored Marcus's wry look, glanced at his watch, and blew out a long breath. "Jesus, it's only ten o'clock! I thought it was at least eleven. I know New Zealand is twelve hours ahead of England but why is time moving so slowly here?"

"Will you stop complaining?" Marcus ran to catch up with him as he headed for the bar to get another drink. "You've been here less than thirty minutes. I've been here since eight."

"Do you want a medal?"

"We promised we'd mingle," Marcus told him.

"I hate mingling."

"Jesus Christ. You've turned into such a fucking old man."

"I am an old man," Cameron said. "I'm fifty-four. You're thirty-two. You're in your prime."

"I don't feel in my prime," Marcus grumbled. "I'm starting to groan like a pensioner when I get up out of a chair."

Cameron laughed and ordered them both a double of Laphroaig, a nice Islay malt. "Have you rung Rebecca tonight?"

"I'll call her when I get back to the room." Marcus accepted the glass from the bartender. "She's going to her Pilates class and then picking Lucy up from daycare, but she'll be back home by one p.m. UK time."

Cameron sipped his drink. "I'm glad she's flying out here on Monday. You shouldn't be away from her for too long."

Marcus rolled his eyes as they wandered away to the edge of the dance floor. "Are you playing marriage counsellor now?"

"I just don't want you to make the same mistakes I did."

Marcus had a gulp of whisky. His eyes were thoughtful, but his tone, when he spoke, was teasing. "Next thing you'll be saying you'd rather be at home with a wife than hooking up with another beautiful blonde."

Cameron had a gulp from his glass. It seared down to his stomach, which burned a little, reminding him that he hadn't eaten since lunch. "If I have enough of these I might be able to make it till midnight," he said, looking ruefully into the glass.

Marcus studied his shoes. "I'm sorry. It's my fault—I made you come here. We should have toured New Zealand a bit, seen some of the sights. Not spent our days cold calling."

Cameron blew out a long breath. Without Marcus's business brain and ability to wheedle money from possible investors, their company wouldn't be in the position it was now. "No, you're right. I have turned into an old man. And anyway, at least the ball is for a good cause." The banners above the buffet tables declared that the ball was in aid of cancer research. Marcus's father had died from bowel cancer a few years ago, so Cameron had agreed to go to support his friend.

"I need some food," he said. "I might scout out the buffet."

"I'll come with you." Marcus joined him as they circled the edge of the dance floor. "They do a nice crab thing in puff pastry."

"That's the stuff that leaves flakes all over your jacket, right?"

"You have to learn to inhale as you take a bite, without choking."

Cameron chuckled. "I'll try one, although I think crab can sometimes…" He stopped walking, his voice trailing off.

Marcus carried on, realized his friend wasn't with him, and turned in confusion. "What?"

Cameron didn't reply. Slowly, Marcus followed his gaze.

About ten feet away, a woman stood on her own, watching the dancers as she sipped from a glass of champagne. She was average height, maybe five seven or eight in a pair of sandals with small heels, and her silver hair suggested she was around Cameron's age, early fifties. She wore an interesting gown in a style he hadn't seen before—it was a silvery-gray, and the thin semi-transparent skirt had a long split up the front and back that parted to reveal gray wide-leg trousers. The bodice was covered with a layer of lace, and she wore a jacket made from the same lace over the top. It was simple, elegant, and yet still sexy, perfect for a woman her age.

But it wasn't the dress that had caught his attention. She'd lifted her mask for a moment to scratch her nose, revealing her face briefly before she lowered the mask again.

"Who is it?" Marcus asked. "Do you know her? Or is the Taylor radar searching out possibilities for the night?"

Cameron felt as if someone had sucked all the air out of the room. "That, my friend," he said softly, "is the woman I loved before my heart turned to the cold, hard piece of stone it is now."

Marcus's eyes widened. "That's Noelle?"

"The one and only."

"Holy shit. Did you know she'd be here?"

"I had no idea. I haven't spoken to her in over thirty years."

The two of them watched her for a long moment as she sipped her champagne, moving a little to the music.

"She's gorgeous," Marcus said. "I wonder what she's doing here? You really didn't know?"

"She moved to New Zealand with her family when she was eighteen. I wasn't even sure if she was still in the country."

"What are the odds?"

"I know." Cameron's head was spinning. Mentions of New Zealand over the years had always made his stomach do a strange little flip. He'd never been, though, up until now, refusing to visit out of a stubborn resentment he'd known was childish but had been unable to control. The country was sparsely populated—only four million people in a land the size of England, which housed sixty-six million souls—but even so, Marcus was right, what were the odds that she'd be here tonight?

"You should ask her to dance," Marcus said.

"I doubt she's here on her own." His pulse raced.

"There's no one with her at the moment."

"She won't remember me."

"You remembered her."

"Maybe her husband's gone to the Gents' or something."

"Jesus, Cam. Just go and talk to her already, will you?" Marcus took Cameron's glass from his hand. "You'll regret it if you don't." Cameron tore his gaze away from her for a moment to look at his friend. Marcus's eyes were bright, encouraging. "Go on," he said. "I'll meet with the Harts and I'll let you know if they want to talk to you. Don't need you scowling at them anyway."

Cameron looked back at Noelle and took a deep breath. "All right." Leaving Marcus to charm the businessmen, he walked up to her.

She glanced at him as he approached and smiled when he stopped before her. "Good evening."

"Good evening." He looked down at her silver mask, into her green eyes. Oh yes, he remembered those so well. "Would you like to dance?"

Her eyes widened, and her lips parted. "Oh. Um…"

He raised his hand, palm uppermost. She looked at it for a moment, and he could see her debating with herself as to whether she should accept. She glanced back at him, and he felt her gaze brush down him, taking in his gray hair and smart suit before returning to his face, making him tingle all over. To his relief she turned, placed her glass on a nearby table, then slid her hand into his.

Backing away, he led her onto the dance floor. He lifted her hand and slid his right onto her hip. The band was playing *Gravity*, the singer doing a reasonable impersonation of John Mayer. "Can you still waltz?" he asked.

"Yes…"

Holding her tightly, he waited for the beat, then began to spin her around. They'd taken dance classes for fun back in England, and had discovered a shared talent they'd both enjoyed. Clearly she hadn't forgotten the steps. For about thirty seconds they danced to the music, relaxing into the rhythm. She moved well, light on her feet, and they spun slowly around the edge of the floor.

"Are you enjoying the ball?" he asked her eventually, conscious that she'd hardly said a word.

"Yes, it's been a lovely evening so far." She moistened her lips with the tip of her tongue. Cameron's pulse increased a bit more.

"Am I stealing you away from anyone?" he asked. "Husband, partner?"

"Just my daughter," she said, and smiled.

"How many children do you have?"

"Two sons and three daughters. One of them brought me here tonight with her partner. He's on the charity's board."

"Five children, that's impressive."

"Do you have kids?" she asked politely.

"Three. Two girls and a boy. I don't see them much."

"That's a shame. I'm lucky enough to see mine all the time. They all live nearby."

"In Auckland?"

"Kerikeri," she said. "In the Northland. It's about three hours away."

"Is it nice up there?"

"It's beautiful. Sub-tropical, a bit like the Mediterranean."

"And... no husband?"

"He died." Her eyes were bright and clear, a beautiful green. "Two years ago this Christmas."

"I'm sorry," he said, meaning it. He felt a sweep of pity for them both, for the lost years, the pain they'd both been through.

She looked at where he was holding her hand, maybe spotting he wore no ring. "Are you here with someone?"

"A business partner. I'm single. My divorce came through six months ago."

"I'm sorry."

"It's okay. It's best this way."

The song wound around them, and for a moment he felt as if there was nobody else in the room. It was as if all the intervening years hadn't existed, and they were back in England, in love, with all the promise of a lifetime of happiness ahead of them.

"Why did you say can you *still* waltz?" she asked suddenly, and he knew she'd been puzzling over his choice of words. "What did you mean?"

He said nothing, heart thumping, waiting for her to make the connection, to work it out.

"Who are you?" she whispered. "I know you. I know I do."

He lifted his hand from her waist to raise his mask.

Her lips parted, her mouth forming an 'O'. "Jesus. Cam?"

She missed a step and stumbled against him. He stopped moving and held her, and they stood motionless in the middle of the dance floor as other couples turned around them, casting them curious glances.

"Hello, Noelle," he said, and smiled.

"What are you doing here?" Her voice was little more than a squeak.

"I'm here on business. We have a meeting in Wellington on Tuesday, but Marcus—my partner—wanted to go to the ball to meet a possible investor. I wasn't going to come. I'm glad I did now."

Someone bumped against them, and he took her hand. "Let's get off the dance floor."

She followed him through the dancers to the edge of the floor and then stood facing him, her eyes wide behind her mask. "I don't believe it," she said. "After all this time."

"I know. How long has it been? Thirty-three years? Thirty-four?"

"A lifetime," she said. She lifted a hand and ran her fingers over his lapel. "You look good. I like your hair."

He ran a hand through it self-consciously. "It's a bit long. It needs a cut."

"I like it. It's a very becoming gray. And that's a nice suit. Italian?"

He nodded and fiddled with the bow tie. "This is so tight it's cutting off my circulation." She smiled, and he lowered his hand, running his gaze down her. "You look amazing."

She glanced at her outfit. "One of my daughters made it."

"Really?"

"She makes wedding dresses for a living and I wanted something for tonight that was appropriate... you know... for my age." She lowered her eyes.

"You look exactly the same as the last time I saw you," he said softly.

She laughed. "Now I know you're lying."

He shook his head. "That *joie de vivre* you always had is still there."

"I don't know. My get-up-and-go has got-up-and-gone," she joked. "I'm feeling my age lately."

But it didn't matter to Cameron that she had fine lines at the edges of her eyes, or that her hair was silver. "I've missed you," he murmured.

I've missed you too. He wanted her to say it, but she didn't.

He checked his watch, then glanced over his shoulder. Marcus was standing talking to two guys in suits, and he nodded as Cameron met his gaze. "I've got to check in with my partner," he said. "But I'd love to catch up more. I don't suppose you'd like to get a drink in the bar?"

She swallowed and looked around her. "Um… I don't know…"

"I'll only be a minute. Don't go anywhere."

Again, she didn't reply. He hesitated, then left her side, circling the dance floor.

His head spun, and his mouth had gone dry. Jesus. After all these years.

Seeing her brought his old feelings back in a rush, tangled up like old boat ropes. Was he doing the right thing in talking to her again?

He reminded himself that he was older and wiser—well, older anyway—and his expectations were lower; he'd learned that affairs of the heart never made him as happy as his work, and he'd filled his life with his business until there wasn't room for anything or anyone else.

He frowned. What did it matter? He was only in New Zealand for a week and then he'd be returning to the UK, back to his busy life. He could spare a few hours to catch up with an old flame.

She might have broken his heart the first time around, but she'd hardly be able to repeat that in an evening.

Chapter Two

Noelle watched Cameron walk away, her heart racing. Her brain was having trouble coping with the knowledge that this was the same man she'd left behind in England all those years ago. Even though his hair was now a becoming steel-gray, he hadn't changed that much. He wasn't overly tall, maybe six foot, but he'd been a swimmer, which had kept him trim and muscular, and the width of his shoulders in the tux and lack of middle-aged paunch over his belt suggested he remained fit. His unusual violet eyes hadn't changed either, and they still gave her the shivers when he looked at her the way he had when she was eighteen, as if he was imagining her naked and picturing all the hot, dirty things he wanted to do to her.

Christ. She was far too old for this. She needed to lie down with a flannel on her forehead and a cup of tea.

"Holy shit, Mum! Who was that?" It was Roberta with her husband, Angus, in tow. She wore a long powder-blue dress and a matching face mask. She'd obviously been watching them, because her curved lips showed her amusement. "Did you see that watch he was wearing? It was a Rolex Deepsea. They're, like, eleven thousand dollars!"

Noelle felt a little faint. "Oh dear."

"Who was he?" Roberta persisted.

"His name is Cameron Taylor."

Roberta stared at her. "English Cameron? Your first boyfriend?"

Noelle nodded.

"Holy fuck."

"Roberta," she scolded automatically, even though she'd been thinking the same thing.

"What's he doing here?" Angus looked across the dance floor to where Cameron was having a conversation with three other men.

"He's here on business. I don't think he's in the country for very long." Her pulse slowed as her brain processed the information. It was a chance meeting, that was all, not the ending to a fairytale. He hadn't moved here. He was visiting, and it sounded as if he was heading south to Wellington soon, while she would be going north back home. It might have blown her brain to see him again, but it didn't mean anything, and there was nothing to get excited about.

"What did he want?" Roberta asked. "Was he just saying hello?"

"Yes... He wants to have a drink in the bar."

"Are you going to?" Angus looked amused.

"I don't know." Noelle felt breathless at the thought of spending more time in Cameron's company. Seeing him had stirred up all the old feelings she'd suppressed over the years, all the guilt at leaving him, the pain of missing him, and the anguish that she'd done the wrong thing that had continued even—if she were honest—after she'd met her husband, Hugh, for a while anyway.

"You should," her daughter stated. "That suit wasn't off the peg."

Noelle knew Roberta was right. His suit was a quality cut and fabric, and it wouldn't have surprised her if it were a Rubinacci, handmade in Naples for a cool five-to-ten thousand dollars. Everything about him said he was wealthy, from his handmade shoes, to the matching Montblanc tie pin and cufflinks, to the silk square tucked into his jacket pocket.

"You've got to go," Roberta persisted. "How often do you get to go on a date with James Bond?"

"One drink in a bar can hardly be called a date," Noelle corrected. But she acknowledged that her daughter was right to compare him to the Fleming hero. Even at the age of twenty there had been something... dangerous about Cameron Taylor, and that certainly hadn't changed. It wasn't just money that he oozed, he also radiated power. He'd asked her for a drink, confident she'd accept. He was a man used to being obeyed.

No wonder he'd been so angry when she'd walked away from him all those years ago.

Part of her wanted to turn now, leg it back to her hotel room, and bury her face in the pillow. Life was good; she missed her husband and she was lonely sometimes, but she was happy enough. She had her family around her, and there would be more grandchildren soon, God willing, and lots to keep her occupied. She didn't need a man to make her complete anymore.

The other half thought about Cameron's violet eyes, and she knew she was fooling herself if she thought she was going to refuse him.

Her pulse started to race again—he'd left the other men and was beginning to walk back around the dance floor toward her. He'd taken off his mask, and he strode with the long confident strides she remembered, always impatient to get where he wanted to be.

"Create a diversion," she told her daughter and son-in-law, removing her own mask. "I need to make a getaway."

"Absolutely not." Roberta spoke firmly. "I don't care if he's only here for the evening. A one-night stand will be the perfect thing to put hairs on your chest."

Noelle blushed with volcanic heat, just in time for him to walk up and pause before her. He surveyed her red face with a hint of a smile before sliding his gaze across to her daughter.

"Good evening," he said, holding out a hand. "I'm Cameron Taylor, and you must be Noelle's daughter."

"Roberta," she said, shaking his hand enthusiastically. "It's lovely to meet you. I've heard so much about you over the years."

"Goodness," Noelle said.

Cameron tried not to laugh. "And you must be Roberta's partner."

"I'm Angus McGregor," Angus said with a grin, shaking his hand.

"It's lovely to meet you all. Would you like to join us in the bar? I suggested to Noelle that we go there for a drink."

Noelle nodded, hopeful they wouldn't abandon her, but Roberta said cheerfully, "Thanks, but I want to dance some more. I don't get much of a chance, so I'm making the most of it!" Taking her partner's hand, she led him away onto the dance floor, Angus giving them an apologetic smile before he spun Roberta into his arms.

Noelle huffed a sigh and looked at where Cameron held out his arm for her to take. "Ready?" he said.

She slipped her hand beneath his elbow, trying not to squeeze her fingers on his biceps. He'd swum most days as a teen—did he still love getting in the water? His firm muscles suggested he did. She felt a little dizzy.

It was just one drink. Surely she could hold it together for that long.

She'd thought he was going to take her over to the bar in the corner, but he led her through the crowd, out of the hall and across the foyer to the separate bar, which was much quieter. "What can I get you?" he asked. "You don't still drink Babycham, I'm guessing?"

She laughed. "A glass of Sauvignon will be great, thank you."

She noticed that when the bartender showed him the wine list, Cameron went straight to the most expensive one and ordered that. He did it casually, obviously used to having the best. Her stomach fluttered. She was hardly poor, but she was used to scanning the menu and choosing a moderately priced wine, to restricting her treats, and to having to save if she wanted a holiday. His family hadn't been rich, that she could remember anyway. Where had he made his money?

He ordered a whisky for himself and leaned on the bar, his eyes on hers as they waited for the drinks.

"So…" he said softly.

She resisted the urge to fidget beneath his steady gaze. "So…"

He smiled. "Don't look so nervous. I want to find out what you've been up to the last thirty years."

It didn't help. Was he going to ask her if she'd thought about him? If she'd regretted the decision she'd made? If he'd featured in her fantasies at all?

"You first," she said nervously.

He accepted the drinks from the bartender and gave his room number. "Shall we sit?" he asked her, picking up his whisky.

She nodded and followed him over to a seat by the window. It was dark out, but someone had strung golden fairy lights around the bar and candles flickered on the table, so the place was lit with a warm glow.

Before he sat, he unbuttoned his jacket, slipped it off, and placed it over the back of the chair. Noelle swallowed a big gulp of wine. He wore a waistcoat over his white shirt, its snug fit showing her he was still slim, although the sleeves of the shirt stretched over his biceps. He'd been gorgeous at twenty and he was gorgeous now, if anything more so, the gray hair lending him a sophistication he hadn't possessed when she'd known him.

Was he still great in bed? She watched him lean back in his chair and sip from his glass. His easy grace and the twinkle in his eye suggested he was. He'd been nineteen when they'd met. She'd been seventeen and he'd been her first, and they'd spent most of the year they'd dated in bed. He'd been insatiable, and she'd been besotted with him. With nothing to compare him to, she'd believed every man to be the same. She knew better now. If she'd known then what she knew now, would she have stayed?

He seemed content to sit there studying her, thinking his own thoughts, his steady gaze making her nervous. He'd been a young man full of quirks, and she was sure that hadn't changed. He had a slight gap between his front teeth. He was ambidextrous. He'd been full of energy when he was younger, his engine always running, continuously tapping on the table or bouncing his leg on the floor. He could do incredible sums in his head, things she couldn't even work out on paper. He'd had an ear for languages and had been studying French and Spanish at the time. He'd adored being in the water—they'd swum a lot when they were young, and he'd enjoyed scuba diving. He'd also loved archaeology and had found fragments of a pot or broken tiles from Roman villas bizarrely captivating. He'd gone on to study the subject at university. Was that what he did now?

He'd also been impatient, occasionally irritable, and confident bordering on arrogant, and he hadn't suffered fools gladly. He'd been larger than life, and when he'd walked into the room it had been like a star going supernova, blinding her so much she hadn't been able to see anything else. She'd orbited around him, in his shadow, and it made her heart race to remember how all-encompassing their relationship had been.

She scolded herself silently for being nervous. She wasn't on trial here. She didn't have to defend her decision to come to New Zealand, and she didn't have to prove that her life had been worthwhile. She'd had a happy marriage, had borne five children, and ran a successful business. Her life had been meaningful; she'd loved and had been loved in return. That was what was important.

"So tell me about yourself," she said, pinning a smile on her face.

"It's hard to know where to start."

"What do you do for a living? You've obviously done well for yourself."

"I run a marine archaeology consultancy firm called Subaqueous."

"Oh, wow! You managed to combine snorkeling and archaeology!"

He grinned. "Yep. Best of both worlds."

"That's amazing." She was genuinely impressed. "And it's obviously doing well?"

"It's the biggest company of its type in northern Europe."

"Jesus."

"Yeah. We take contracts all over the world now. Including New Zealand."

"You must have worked incredibly hard to be so successful."

He sighed. For the first time she saw signs of the passing years in his face, lines around his eyes and mouth, frown lines on his forehead. Each line told a story, she thought, of something in his life that had frustrated him.

"When you left," he said, "I had no interest in settling down. I admit I was angry, back then." He stated it as a fact, without accusation. "I threw myself into finishing my degree, took a postgrad in marine research and a masters in public affairs with a focus on submerged cultural research management. Archaeological jobs are hard to come by, and I felt I needed a fallback, so I took courses on scientific diving, economics, management, sustainable development…" His lips curved up. "Stop me if I'm boring you."

"No, no, I find it fascinating," she said truthfully. "Your company's based in England?"

"London, yes. It started small and grew very gradually until I met Marcus, my business partner, ten years ago. He was fresh out of university, green as a cucumber, and with one of the brightest minds for business I'd ever seen. He saw the potential of Subaqueous immediately. With him behind the wheel, we've gone from strength to strength and expanded exponentially. I'm all about the archaeology and the environment, and he runs the business now. It's the perfect marriage."

She smiled. "So you've worked on some interesting projects?"

His eyes lit up. "We've studied shipwrecks all around the coast of Europe, and looked at everything from prehistoric sites right up to modern day. Although the Mary Rose—Henry VIII's flagship—was raised in 1982, I worked on a second round of excavations in 2004. That was cool. And because I speak Spanish, I've worked in South America a lot, on the Sunken Ships of Colombia project, the Lost Ships of Henry Morgan project in Panama… Far too many to name."

"So why New Zealand? What's drawn you here?"

"We've put in a bid to do the excavation of a large Maori canoe—I think you call it a *waka*?—found over at the Hokianga. I'm not quite sure where that is—an area on the west coast, I think? There's talk that it might have belonged to Kupe, so of course it would have great significance to New Zealand. It's getting a lot of attention in the world of archaeology."

Noelle's eyes widened. Kupe was supposedly a great chief from the mythical land of Hawaiki who discovered New Zealand long before the Europeans. In the mythology of some Maori tribes, he'd arrived in the tenth century, which placed him hundreds of years before the known founding canoes of the thirteenth century. "Do you think you'll win the bid?"

"Possibly. Marcus is good at charming his way into projects. We'll probably share the excavation with the Maritime Archaeological Association of New Zealand—they'll drive the project, but we'll be able to source a good deal of funding, and I don't think they'll be able to say no to that."

"Would you be doing the excavation yourself?"

His eyes met hers. "No," he said softly. "I'm involved with a big project off the coast of Cartagena in Colombia, raising a Spanish galleon called the San Jose."

"That sounds interesting," she said politely.

"I'm always telling people we're not treasure hunters," he said, "but the San Jose is called the Holy Grail of shipwrecks because of all the gold doubloons and silver and emeralds it's supposed to have had as cargo. If that turns out to be the case, it'll be worth a billion dollars." He grinned at her startled look. "Not to me personally. But it'll still pay well."

Noelle nodded, what little peak of excitement she'd had at the thought of him coming to New Zealand dying at the news that he wouldn't be returning there to work.

This really was a chance to reconnect, maybe to put any ghosts to rest. She'd thought about him so often over the years and wondered how he was doing. It was a nice opportunity to talk about old times, that was all.

She had another mouthful of wine, letting the tension flow out of her body. He was an old friend, and it was fascinating to hear what he'd been up to all this time. "So that's your business," she said. "What about your personal life?"

Chapter Three

Cameron swirled the whisky over the ice in the glass. Had Noelle asked whether he'd be returning to work here because she wanted to see him again? He looked down at the amber liquid and stifled a sigh. It didn't matter either way. He wasn't coming back, and she'd made it clear many years ago that he wasn't high on her list of priorities.

Maybe he shouldn't have gone over to talk to her and started off this chain reaction of regret and longing. But it was done now, and besides, it was good to be with her again, even if he knew it was only temporary.

He finished off the whisky in his glass. "I need another drink before I tell you that tale." He rose and went over to the barman, ordered another round, and brought the glasses back to the table.

"I shouldn't have any more," Noelle said as he put her drink in front of her. "I've already had two glasses of champagne, and a glass of wine. I need to keep my wits about me."

He sat and rolled his eyes. "I think we're old enough not to have to worry about that."

"You're here on business," she reminded him. "How would the deal go if you started doing your Travolta impersonation?"

He grinned, remembering a time when he'd done just that, one night in London. It had been the week after Christmas, after her eighteenth birthday, and they'd celebrated by going to a club for the first time. If he remembered correctly, he'd taken her back to his room on the university campus where he was studying, and as soon as they'd walked in, she'd stripped off her dress, and they'd had amazing sex right there, up against the door.

Noelle's face had gone an attractive shade of pink. So, she remembered too.

"That was a good night," he said.

"You're a wicked man," she murmured, sipping her wine.

"Those were great days."

"We were very young," she stated.

"Yes, we were."

"A lot has changed since then."

He sighed. "Tell me about it."

"I think it's still your turn."

He gave a wry smile. It was warm in the bar, and he felt restricted and hot in his clothing. He tugged his bow tie undone with relief, leaving the ends to hang, and undid the top button, then took out his cufflinks and slowly rolled up his shirt sleeves a few times. Noelle watched him, her green eyes steady, her expression difficult to decipher.

How much should he tell her? Or, more importantly perhaps, should he hold anything back? There was no point, really. He had nothing to hide. If this were any other night, and she were any other woman in a bar, he'd turn on the charm and try out a few lines, but that wasn't what this was about.

"I didn't have a steady relationship for a long time after you left," he said. "I gave a hundred-and-ten percent of my life to my job, and there wasn't room for anyone else."

"I can't imagine you were a monk." Her eyes glittered.

His lips curved up. "No…"

His mind strayed back to the first time he'd seen her. It had been at the local swim club. She'd stood on the diving board and done a perfect 360 dive, which had impressed him almost as much as her stunning figure in the navy-blue swimsuit. After watching her swim flawless lengths for thirty minutes, he'd climbed out of the pool, changed at the speed of light, and waited for her in the adjoining café, where he'd asked her to join him for a drink. He'd been nineteen; she'd been seventeen and beautiful, and he'd fallen for her immediately. She'd also been a virgin, and he'd taken great joy in introducing her to the delights of sex. She'd been open to everything he'd suggested with a few ideas of her own, and she'd been wild and spirited, exciting and adventurous. He'd thought they'd be together forever.

When she'd announced that her father had taken a job on the other side of the world in New Zealand, he'd assumed she'd stay in England. When she'd told him she was considering going, he'd done everything he could to persuade her to stay, but in the end she'd chosen her parents over him.

The apparent ease with which she'd made her choice had crushed him. Adult Cameron knew it couldn't have been that simple for her, but the young Cam had taken it as a personal slight. He'd been devastated and had covered it with indignant fury, and they hadn't parted well. The resentment had taken years to burn off. Sometimes it still simmered in his gut. She was the only woman he'd ever truly loved. Not that he was about to tell her that.

He took a mouthful of whisky, then sighed silently. *Grow up, Cameron.*

"I met Lara on my thirtieth birthday," he said. "I was in a bar with some mates, and she was there with her friends. We all ended up in one big group, and I got talking to her." He'd actually ended up taking her back to his place, but he decided to keep that detail to himself. "She was unlike anyone I'd met before. We didn't have anything in common, and I suppose that should have been a warning sign, but at the time I found it refreshing. I was involved with archaeology all day every day, and so was everyone around me. But Lara was... different. She was a chef, and she loved food—buying it, cooking it, eating it. She held a vegetable the way I hold a piece of Samian ware, as if it was fascinating, precious. She was ambitious and driven, and she had a busy life of her own, which suited me fine; she wasn't hanging around, wondering where I was every minute of the day. The relationship worked well, at the time, or at least I thought it did. We married a year later, and then had three children over the next six or seven years."

"What are their names?"

"Rosie is twenty-three, Josh is twenty-one, and Stella is nineteen." He turned the whisky glass in his fingers. "I wasn't a good father."

Noelle's expression softened. "I don't believe that for one minute."

"That's nice of you to say, but it's the truth. When the kids were young I was working day and night, trying to get Subaqueous off and running. Then when they were in their teens I met Marcus, and things took off. We were so busy in those early years—there weren't enough hours in the day. There was always something more important to do than pick up the kids from daycare or watch them prancing around at ballet lessons. I missed everything, and I didn't realize it until it was too late."

Her eyes were full of pity. "What happened with Lara?"

"At the time, I didn't notice the marriage disintegrating. We'd never been close in the way that other couples seemed to be. I don't know if that was entirely my fault. She blamed me, but I don't remember her ever begging me to come home, or saying once that she missed me. Looking back, it was a marriage of convenience. She had her life and I had mine, and I thought both of us were content with that. I knew she had lovers when I was away and it didn't bother me. I was never short of company." He was conscious of Noelle's gaze on him, but he kept his eyes on his glass. "Then, three years ago, she rang me one day, out of the blue, and told me she'd had enough and wanted a divorce."

Noelle's eyebrows rose. "Ouch."

"Yeah. I was in the middle of a huge project, but I cancelled it and came home. We talked for a whole week on and off. It all came pouring out. How lonely she was, how inattentive I'd been. How she'd had to do everything for the kids. To be honest, I was more baffled than anything. I'd thought she was happy. What an idiot." He stopped, conscious of the harsh tone in his voice.

"What happened?" she asked.

"I said I wanted to try to make it work. That I'd spend more time at home. I tried for about two months. But it was clear it was pointless. When we were together all the time, we realized we had nothing in common. We argued constantly. Neither of us was happy. And in the end, I left. She filed for divorce a week later. The kids took her side, and fair enough, I suppose. They knew how little I'd been around for both them and their mother. I failed them all, I know that. I only have myself to blame."

He could imagine what Noelle was thinking. She'd probably pictured him all these years happily married, never giving her a second thought. She'd have no idea how much he'd missed her, and how no woman he'd met had lived up to her. Or how angry and bitter that had made him.

His throat tightened. Embarrassed, he had a mouthful of whisky, then regretted it as his stomach burned.

At that moment Marcus appeared at the doorway to the bar, spotted him, and came over. He carried a plate of food, and he put it on the table in front of Cameron. "You've got to eat something," he scolded.

Cameron gave him a wry look. "Noelle, this is my mother, Marcus Brant."

She smiled and held out her hand, and Marcus shook it. "It's wonderful to meet you," Marcus told her. "I've heard so much about you."

She glanced at Cameron, who shrugged, and then she smiled at his friend. "Cam's been telling me all about Subaqueous. It sounds as if you've done an amazing job."

"If only he'd picked a name that was easier to spell, it would have been perfect."

She laughed, and Cameron grinned. "How did it go with the Harts?" he asked.

"Yep, they're in. That's another two hundred grand in the pot."

Cameron nodded. If they didn't get the contract with that sort of financial backing, he'd be very surprised. "Well done."

"Now I'm off to bed," Marcus said. "I'm going to ring Rebecca. See you in the morning."

"All right, mate. Sleep well. Give her my love."

Marcus backed away. "Make sure he eats," he told Noelle before he disappeared out of the door. "He's got a stomach ulcer."

Cameron glared at him, then blew out a breath as she raised her eyebrows.

"Is that true?" she asked.

"No."

"Cam…"

"I get heartburn sometimes, mainly because I skip meals when I'm busy. Marcus is an old woman."

"It's good to know someone's looking after you." She pushed the plate toward him. "Eat up, then."

He gave in, picked up one of the crab puffs that Marcus had mentioned earlier, and ate it. His stomach rumbled approvingly.

"You shouldn't drink on an empty stomach," she said. "That'll only make it worse."

"Yes, Mum."

"I'm used to playing the motherly role. It comes easily."

He smiled. "So, five kids," he said. "What are their names?"

"Dominic's the eldest—he's a deacon now."

"A deacon? I don't remember you being very religious."

"It's mainly Hugh's influence," she clarified. "My late husband. He went to church every Sunday. He never forced the kids to go with him, but Dominic used to want to go. His wife was religious too, but she died, and I think that had an effect on him, because he decided he didn't want to be a priest. He's a counsellor at the high school, and he does a lot of stuff in the community. He's a good boy."

"And your other kids?"

"Elliot's my second, he's a cop. Roberta—you met her—she runs a café. Phoebe and Bianca are twins, and they make the wedding dresses. They're the youngest at twenty-seven."

"What do you do?" He took a bite out of a small club sandwich.

"I run the bridal shop." She sipped her wine. "When my father died, he left me and his grandchildren money. Hugh and I decided to invest it in a shop, because Phoebe and Bianca were so obviously talented with their dressmaking. They've won awards at the World of Wearable Arts Exhibition."

His eyebrows rose. "That's impressive."

"They're good, and I'm not just saying that. We're making a name for ourselves in the North Island. Next stop the world." She smiled.

"Tell me about Hugh," he said.

Chapter Four

Noelle's smile faded, and she turned her glass around in her fingers. Cameron's tale about his ex-wife had unsettled her. She didn't want to know that he'd been unhappy all these years. That he'd had affairs, and had been an absent father. Was he saying it was her fault? That her leaving had been the reason for his unhappiness? Surely not. She'd been eighteen. How could she have known that her decision would have such an impact on their lives?

"What do you want to know?" she asked, a tad resentfully. She didn't want to talk about her placid, faithful, quiet husband to this man. To have him mock her because they'd both know she'd settled for comfort and security over passion.

"Where did you meet him?" he wanted to know.

"I'd been here a year, and I'd gone to college and done a few business courses, but I wasn't sure what I wanted to do. I saw an advert for a business manager for a small construction firm and applied. He was the owner and he interviewed me, and I think I knew right away that he liked me. He was a few years older, and he was a good man, kind, and generous."

She stopped. She wanted to tell Cam that her life had been full of adventure, that Hugh had been exciting and passionate, and that they'd set the bedsheets alight, but it would have been a lie. In a way Hugh's calmness and gentleness had attracted her because he'd been so different from the man she'd left behind. She'd not wanted someone to take Cam's place. She'd wanted someone to wipe away his memory so it didn't hurt anymore. It hadn't worked, but she'd been happy with Hugh, happy enough that she'd never even looked at another man in all the years they'd been married.

"It's okay," Cameron said.

"I loved him," she said fiercely. "And I miss him every day."

"Noelle." He put a hand on hers. "It's okay. I'm not about to get mad because you found someone who made you happy."

She stared at where his hand rested on hers, her fingers tingling from his touch. He withdrew it and leaned back.

"He's been the only man in my life since I came here," she said.

"You've not dated anyone since he died?"

"No."

"Why not?"

She gave him an odd look. "That's a strange question. He was my husband. He died."

"I thought you said it was two years ago."

"Not quite two years," she said, a defensive tone creeping into her voice.

His expression softened. "I admire your loyalty. And I'm not belittling your feelings for your husband of three decades. I'm... surprised. You're gorgeous. Fun. Naughty." He smiled. "I'm shocked that you haven't been snapped up again."

His description embarrassed her. "I'm neither fun nor naughty."

He pursed his lips. "That's not what I remember." And there it was again, the look in his eyes that told her he was remembering things she'd said, things she'd done. Intimate things. With him.

She looked at her glass and lifted it to take a big swallow. She didn't want to think about what life would have been like if she'd stayed in England. She was a mother of five children with a respectable business and a happy life. She didn't need an old, bad boyfriend waltzing in—literally—reminding her what she'd lost.

"I've upset you," he said.

She met his gaze. He looked contrite. She sighed. She might as well be honest with him. What was the point in hiding her feelings after all this time, when he'd blown into her life like a leaf on the wind, and he was going to disappear so soon in the same way?

"It's odd," she said, "seeing you again after all these years. I hadn't forgotten what we had, but I've done my very best not to think about it, because I didn't want to spend my whole life filled with regret."

He studied her for a long time, emotions passing behind his amazing violet eyes like fish in a tank. "You do have regrets, then?" he asked eventually.

Her brow furrowed. "Of course I have regrets. Did you really think I didn't?" His face told her that was exactly what he thought. He was convinced she'd left England without looking back.

She held her breath, shocked into silence. For God's sake... She'd told him at the time what a terrible decision it had been to have to make, but he'd taken it as a sign that she didn't love him enough.

That hadn't been the reason. Her parents had begged her to go with them and, as their only child, she'd known she'd miss them terribly. Their love and support was unconditional and guaranteed. But the love of the impatient, fiery young man? That had held no such assurances.

She'd known even then how ambitious he was, how driven. She'd been eighteen and, deep down, she'd been certain she wouldn't be enough for him. He'd never suggested going with her. She'd thought he'd mourn her for a few months, then find himself another girl and forget all about her by the end of the year.

It looked as if she'd been very, very wrong.

A small part of her wanted to yell at him for being such an idiot. But the rest of her felt a deep sense of overwhelming sorrow and pity.

One night, when they were lying in the dark not long after they met, he'd told her that his mother had taken her own life when he was eight years old. She thought about his words regarding his ex-wife, *I don't remember her ever begging me to come home, or saying once that she missed me.* He must have felt as if all the women in his life abandoned him, as if none of them ever loved him enough to stay. It made her want to cry.

She took his hand in hers. "Hugh was my companion, the rock by my side, and I'll never wish that I hadn't met him. But you... Cam, you were the love of my life. Hugh knew that. He once told me he knew there was a place in my heart reserved for you that would never be his." It had made her cry at the time, and tears pricked her eyes now. "But he was okay with that. We had many, many happy years together, and I was faithful to him. Even in my heart, I made sure of that. I never wished he was you when we were together. It was only when I was alone that I opened that sealed box in my heart and let you out."

Cameron took a big swallow of whisky, looking away, out of the window into the darkness. Noelle felt a kind of tired relief now she'd told the truth. She wasn't being disrespectful to her husband. Hugh had been a good man, and she'd brought up his children, cared for him, and made him a comfortable home. She'd been devoted to him in every way, loyal, faithful, supportive, and she'd missed him dreadfully when he died. How she felt about him had no bearing on how she felt about the man whose fingers now curled around her own.

"I didn't leave because I didn't love you enough," she said softly. "Back then going to New Zealand was viewed as a one-way trip. Flights were expensive, and it wasn't the same as it is today. People who emigrated came back so rarely, and I couldn't bear to think I might never see my parents again. I couldn't give them up for a young man who I knew wanted to conquer the world. I didn't think I'd be enough for you."

He gave a short, humorless laugh.

"You find it amusing now," she said, "but you've told me the story of how you were relieved that your wife didn't make demands on you. That you had separate lives. What would have happened if we'd stayed together? Would you have given up your dreams? Would you still have had affairs as you jet-setted around the world?"

He removed his hand from hers and sat back, rubbing his chest with a motion that told her he had heartburn again.

"Eat a sandwich," she said.

"I've had enough." He pushed the plate away.

She leaned her forearms on the table. It was all out in the open now, everything laid bare. She felt a sense of lightness, as if someone had come along and removed the heavy overcoat she'd been wearing for years that had weighed her down without her realizing it.

She wasn't to blame for the mistakes he'd made in his life. She'd made her choices and he'd made his. She'd been happy, and he could have been too, except that he'd let his stubbornness and resentment overwhelm him. That wasn't her fault. It had been an impossible decision for an eighteen-year-old to make, and if she were to do it again, she knew she'd make the same choice. She wished he'd accepted it, though, and found someone who had made him happy.

"How many affairs have you had?" she asked. "Over the years?"

His eyebrows rose. "What?"

"I just wondered. You really think your wife knew?"

"I know she did."

"Did you sleep with someone else first, or did she?"

He turned his glass in his fingers. "She did. It was a few years after Stella was born. I got back from a trip and Lara told me, straight out, that she'd been seeing someone. She looked me in the eye and said, 'That's not a problem, is it?' And I thought right, that's how it's going to be. I was puzzled at the time how little it affected me, to be honest. If anything, I felt relieved."

"Relieved?"

"If she had lovers, I saw that as her giving me permission to have them, too. I was away a lot, I was often... lonely. Next time I traveled, I met a woman in the bar, asked her up to my room, and that was that."

"So how many?" she asked.

He laughed and ran a hand through his hair. "I don't know. A few I guess, over the years."

"Were any of them serious?"

"Not really. Occasionally they lasted a few weeks if I was staying in the same place. At other times they were one-offs."

"One-night stands."

"Yes." His eyes gleamed. "You can't imagine that, can you?"

"What do you mean?"

"Picking up a guy you've never met before in a bar, taking him back to your room, and having sex with him."

"Jesus. I can't think of anything more horrific."

They both started laughing. "I don't believe that," he said.

"I'm not the same girl I was," she said wryly.

"I don't believe that, either."

She sipped her wine. "I'm fifty-two, Cam."

"I know. But you're not going to tell me that you don't like sex anymore, because I definitely won't believe that."

She scratched at a mark on the table. "It's not that. At eighteen, everything was about sex. It consumes you at that age; it's all you think about."

"It's certainly all we thought about."

Her face warmed, and she refused to look up at him. He'd been gentle with her the first time, and he'd never been rough exactly, but he'd always been very... enthusiastic. He'd wanted her everywhere, outside, on the beach, behind trees, in the bathrooms of people's houses, everywhere they could scrape a few minutes alone. He'd delighted in showing her every position he could think of, and researching some new ones with her, and he'd always made sure she had an orgasm or three. He'd wanted to try everything, and she'd been more than happy to comply. The memories made her head spin.

She sighed. "But things happen to a woman as she gets older. She changes physically, emotionally. Plus I've had five children."

"I've had three," he said. They both laughed again.

"I'm not about to go stripping off my clothes and baring my stretch marks to a complete stranger," she said.

"Fair enough," he replied, although his eyes suggested he didn't think that would be such a bad idea.

She frowned, not liking his unspoken implication that she was missing out. "I've come to accept it's not a big part of my life anymore." If she were honest, it hadn't been for many years. Despite having fathered five children, Hugh's sex drive had never been as high as hers, but she wasn't going to tell Cam that. "I've learned to channel that energy elsewhere."

"Like?"

Her lips twitched. "Kneading bread dough or working in the garden."

He chuckled. "Life in the fast lane, eh?"

"It's amazing how much energy you can burn off digging the veggie patch."

They smiled at each other. "I know we're supposed to live in an equal opportunities world," she said, "but it's not the same for women, I don't care what anyone says. I can't go into a bar, pick up a guy, and take him back for sex. For a start, it's dangerous."

His smile faded. "Yeah, I get that."

"Young women seem to think there's no problem with having multiple partners, but I wasn't brought up like that. I like sex, but only in a committed relationship. I don't want to sleep with men I don't know."

"I understand. How about men you used to know but haven't seen in a while?"

Chapter Five

Noelle's jaw actually dropped like a character in a cartoon. He wouldn't have been shocked if her eyes had fallen out on springs.

"Oh, come on," he said. "You walked into that one."

She blushed. "Don't tease me."

"I'm not. Well, only a little bit." He gave her an amused, exasperated look. "The hottest girl I've ever been with walks into my life for the night—I'm hardly going to look the other way."

She studied his face, her lips slowly curving up. "You're serious."

"Of course I'm serious. I've got a nice suite waiting for us upstairs. Shall we go?"

He was half-serious. If she'd said yes, he'd have taken her hand and led her up there right now. But he knew that wasn't going to happen. She wasn't the sort of woman to have one-night stands, that much was clear. It was a fantasy, and they both knew it.

She smiled. "You're incorrigible."

"I'm also going to have another drink. You want one?"

He expected her to refuse, but she hesitated and looked up at the bottles above the bar, then said, "I'll have a brandy. I'm guessing you won't let me buy a round."

He waved a hand, rose, ordered the drinks, and brought them back, pleased she wasn't leaving yet. It was past eleven o'clock now, and although the music continued to echo from the ballroom, in the foyer he could see people making their way up to their rooms.

"Tell me more about your children," she said.

He told her about Rosie currently studying to be a GP, about Josh following in his mother's footsteps and training to be a chef, and about Stella, who'd started an engineering course at university.

"So none of them are interested in joining Subaqueous?" she asked.

"No," he said sadly. "I should have taken them swimming and scuba diving more, or brought them with me on excavations, but I was always too busy." It was his second-greatest regret.

"Are any of them married?" Noelle asked.

"No. They all have partners. Difficult to say how serious they are."

"So you're not a grandfather yet?"

He pulled a face, and she laughed. "Don't know that I'm ready to be a grandad," he said. "What about you. Are you a grandmother?"

"Yes. Dominic has a daughter, Emily, by his first wife who died, and I suspect there'll be one by his second wife on the way soon. Elliot's broken up with his girlfriend, so he'll be a while. I expect Roberta and Angus will start a family soon, although they're not getting married until January."

"And the twins?"

"Bianca's settling down with her fella. The next one to have a baby will hopefully be Phoebe." She told him about her daughter's accident, explaining how the girl had lost her memory for a while, and how she'd struggled to fall pregnant. "We thought she was going to have to have IVF, but out of the blue it happened. She's only ten weeks, so it's early days, but she had her first scan last week and there was a heartbeat, so we're hopeful."

She was surrounded by her friends and family, he thought, half-envious of her. He'd always told himself that a career and excitement were more important, but he was no longer sure. They were different. His life was fulfilling and busy, but Noelle sounded *happy*.

"What about your parents?" he asked, as that had been the reason she'd left England.

"Mum died eight years ago from breast cancer. That was difficult. Dad was never quite the same without her. But he'd worked hard, and he had a busy life. He'd done well for himself. He died five years ago."

"And then your husband passed away," Cameron said. "How did he die, if you don't mind me asking?"

"A heart attack. He was on his own, so it's possible that if someone had been there, he might have survived." She looked at her glass and swallowed. "But anyway, he didn't. It was a shock, although looking back, more of a shock than it should have been. You read all the time about the dangers, and I used to tell him not to put salt on his food and to watch his fat intake and do more exercise, but men think they're immortal, don't they? They never think it's going to happen to them." She looked pointedly at Cameron's stomach.

"It's just heartburn," he said, amused.

"You have to take care of yourself. Promise me?"

"I promise," he said, although he knew he wouldn't change his ways. That was a new trick, and he was a very old dog.

"Tell me more about your business," she said. "Working on the Mary Rose must have been so exciting."

He could talk for hours about Subaqueous and not run out of steam. He tried to tell himself not to get carried away and bore her, but she kept asking questions and she seemed genuinely interested, so in the end he relaxed, and they talked for a long time about places he'd been and the jobs he'd done.

She didn't want another alcoholic drink, so in the end they ordered a couple of coffees and sipped them slowly as they finished off the plate of food that Marcus had brought, talking about all things under the sun. She told him about her life in New Zealand, about how her kids had grown up fishing, surfing, and playing on the beach. "They didn't wear shoes until they went to high school," she said, laughing. "Can you imagine that?"

Cameron thought about the private schools he'd sent his children to, and how horrified the teachers would have been if the kids had stripped off their leather shoes and pristine white socks. "Not really."

She gave him a thoughtful look. "It's not too late, you know."

His heart skipped a beat. "For what?"

"To get to know your children."

He blew out a breath. "I suppose. Don't get me wrong; we're not enemies or anything. I call them once a week, and I see them occasionally when I'm in London. But I have no influence on their lives. They don't consult me if they have a decision to make. They don't confide in me. I don't think that will change no matter how much effort I make."

"It might."

He didn't reply. It was only when the divorce was going through that Josh had admitted Lara had spent a lifetime telling them how their father had failed them. Josh, at least, had tried to think for himself, and made his own efforts to keep in contact with his dad. But Cameron's girls were cool and distant, and he knew he'd never be able to undo what their mother had whispered in their ears.

Noelle glanced up at the clock above the bar, and her eyebrows rose. "It's gone midnight! Wow. I can't remember the last time I was up so late."

"You always used to be a night bird," he said, remembering the evenings they'd lain awake, hot and sticky in the bed after their lovemaking, listening to the rain.

"Oh, I still am. I don't fall asleep until one or two in the morning. But I'm usually reading or watching TV—I don't go out much at this time of night."

"I told Marcus I'd turn into a pumpkin," he said.

She chuckled. "That was the carriage, not Cinderella."

"He did point out that clearly I don't have young children anymore." Not that he would ever have known the details of the fairytales. He'd never seen a Disney movie in his life. "You had a lucky escape," he said impulsively, making her eyebrows rise. "All these years I've thought that you made the wrong decision, but I can see now that you made the right one. You've had a loving husband, and all your family around you. That's good. I'm happy for you."

Her expression softened. "I wonder how different things would have been if I'd stayed. I wonder if we'd still be together."

He didn't reply, because even though he was convinced he would have been faithful to her, she would never believe him.

"I'd better go to bed," she said softly.

Reluctantly, he rose from the table, slid on his jacket, and held out his hand. She looked at it, smiled, and slipped hers into it, and slowly they began to walk out of the bar and across the foyer. The music had stopped, and people were heading out of the hotel or up to their rooms. They waited for an elevator, went in with four or five other people when the doors opened, and she pressed the button for the fifth floor.

The doors closed, and the elevator rose. Cameron's heart pounded on his ribs. It couldn't end like this. Meeting up with her had been a chance in a million. How could he let her walk away from him again?

The elevator stopped at floor three and two people got off before it began to rise again. Noelle stood beside him quietly, her hand still in his. Her green eyes held sadness and regret.

"I suppose we should say goodbye," she said.

The elevator reached floor five, and the doors slid open.

Cameron walked forward, bringing her with him, and led her out of the elevator and into the corridor. The doors slid closed, and then they were alone.

The corridor was quiet, and they were half in shadow from the dim lighting.

He turned to her and cupped her face. "Can I kiss you?"

Her lips parted, but no words came out. A frown flickered on her brow. He wondered whether she was fighting with herself as to whether it would be disloyal to her husband. Her green eyes studied his face. Waiting was the hardest thing he'd ever had to do, but he forced himself to stand still.

Then, finally, she gave the tiniest nod.

Pleasure swept through him, and he lowered his lips to hers.

Her mouth was soft, her lips cool. She placed her hands on his chest and for a moment he thought she was going to push him away, but then she slid her hands under his jacket, around his waist, and he sighed and wrapped his arms around her. He touched his tongue to her lips and she welcomed it with a thrust of her own, and they exchanged a long, sensual kiss.

When he eventually lifted his head, there was a dreamy look in her eyes.

"Noelle," he murmured, sliding a hand into her silver hair.

"I've missed you," she whispered.

"I've missed you too." He kissed her again. "Come back to my room with me."

She inhaled, her eyes widening.

"It's just one night," he said. "For old time's sake."

She swallowed. "I can't."

"Why not?"

"Cameron... I'm fifty-two."

He laughed. "I'm fifty-four."

"I know, but... I haven't been with anyone for so long..."

"I'll help you oil the rusty parts." He nuzzled her ear.

"Oh Jesus." She pushed him away. "I really can't. What would my kids say?"

"Don't tell them," he said, amused.

She didn't have an answer for that. He could see this whole scenario was completely alien to her. In her mind she was a mother and a grandmother, a business woman, a respected pillar of the community. Having a one-night stand didn't fit into that image at all.

"Come on." He pulled her close again. "We were so good together. Do you remember Valentine's Day?"

She lowered her eyelids, and he knew she was remembering the evening. He'd bought her a box of chocolates and had spent the evening letting them melt on various parts of her body before licking them off. They'd had to wash the sheets afterward, but it had been worth it.

"It was a long time ago," she whispered.

"Don't you want me?" He lifted her chin so he could look into her eyes. "Don't you want to see if it's still as good as it used to be?"

"You'd be disappointed in me."

"Never." He kissed her. "Come to bed with me, Noelle. Let me love you again, just for one night. You owe me that."

It was the wrong thing to say. Her eyes hardened, and she moved back. "I don't owe you anything."

"I didn't mean—"

"It's been a nice evening," she said, "and it was lovely to see you again. I mean that. But… I can't."

She tore herself away from his hands and ran away, along the corridor, without looking back. She turned the corner, and a few moments later he heard a door open and close, and then everything fell silent again.

He remembered what he'd thought at the beginning of the night, that she wouldn't be able to break his heart a second time.

Wrong again, he thought.

Chapter Six

Monday, 4 p.m.

Noelle finished serving a customer, asked a woman browsing the rack of gowns to shout if she needed any help, then went into her office and sat at her desk.

She picked up a pile of invoices, leafed through them, then leaned back in her chair and dropped them back onto the desk.

An unusual listlessness settled over her. She was not normally a woman who gave in to moods. Going through the menopause was a trial at times, but she'd been determined not to let it get the better of her. She took supplements and ate well, exercised frequently, and if she felt irritable or fed up, she took herself off to the garden and worked on the veggie patch, then had a soak in the hot tub with a glass of wine and a piece of chocolate. Invariably she felt better afterward.

So today was unusual, although not unexpected. Walking away from Cameron on Saturday night had been the hardest thing she'd ever had to do. She'd gone into her hotel room, sat on the bed, and burst into tears. She'd then turned and sobbed into her pillow, crying for the years she'd missed with him, and wishing with all her heart that she'd been brave enough to take him up on his offer.

After a while, though, the tears had dried, and she'd lain there realizing it would never have happened. She was fifty-two, a mother and a grandmother, and she was not the sort of person to have a one-night stand, even if she had known the guy. Wild sex was simply not a part of her life anymore. As sad as that was, it was what happened in life. Priorities change. Nobody has sex at fifty the way they do at eighteen. Her husband had died, and it was nobody's fault, and she had to learn to get on with her life and give thanks for all the wonderful things she still had.

She couldn't deny that some hot sex would have been great, though.

She poked at the remains of her lunch on her desk, thought about getting up to ask Roberta for a coffee, then heard her daughters' voices coming from the shop. They were whispering, but she could hear odd phrases, "She's really upset…" "Maybe we should say something…" "What do you think happened?"

On Sunday morning she'd missed breakfast and had texted Roberta to say she'd meet her at the car at ten. Roberta and Angus had been there with bright grins, obviously assuming she'd stayed with Cameron, but their smiles had faded rapidly as they'd seen the sadness in her eyes.

"No, I didn't stay the night with him," she snapped uncharacteristically, and she'd gotten in the car and hardly said a word all the way back.

She sighed. She'd never given her children a reason to worry about her. When Hugh died, she'd managed her grief privately, ensuring she was there for her kids, especially Phoebe, who'd taken her father's death so very hard.

And she'd never done anything to shock them. She'd never gotten a tattoo, or dyed her hair purple, or taken a lover, or declared she was going to Africa to help build houses like one of her friends had. A little part of her had despised people who hit middle-age and bought sports cars or had facelifts, trying to fight against the fact that they were growing old. She'd been determined to age gracefully, and she didn't want her girls to start worrying about her now.

She pushed herself to her feet and went into the shop. "Hello my darlings," she said, smiling as Roberta, Bianca, and Phoebe turned rather guiltily. "Please don't be worried about me. I'm fine."

The girls exchanged glances. "Are you sure?" Phoebe said. "You've been very quiet all day."

"What happened at the ball, Mum?" Bianca asked. "Roberta said you had a drink with Cameron. Did he upset you?"

"No, no, not in the way you mean, anyway. It was just strange seeing him again after all these years. A bit unsettling, you know? It's okay, it'll pass."

"I can't believe he was there," Phoebe said. "It must have been such a shock."

"Just a bit, yes."

Bianca glanced at Roberta, then back at her mother. "Did he ask you to go back to his room?"

Noelle's face warmed at the thought of discussing this with her daughters. She'd told them about Cameron a long time ago, one evening when they were teens and they were all painting their toenails and talking about boys. She had no secrets from her kids, but that didn't mean she was comfortable discussing her sex life. "I think that's private, don't you?"

"I know he did," Roberta said. "He couldn't take his eyes off you. Why didn't you go, Mum?"

Noelle's cheeks burned even hotter. "I wouldn't do that."

"Why?" Phoebe wanted to know.

"Your father…" she began.

"I told you," Bianca said to her sisters. "Mum, you know it would be okay with us if you were to start dating again, right?"

"We want you to be happy," Phoebe said, her eyes shining. Noelle could only imagine how difficult it was for her to say. "And we don't expect you to stay alone for the rest of your life."

Roberta gave her mother an impatient look. "If you were seventy-two, I suppose I could understand it, although I still don't think there's a reason that any person can't find love again, no matter what their age. But you're only fifty-two! Do you really want to be alone for the next thirty years?"

Noelle's throat tightened, and tears pricked her eyes.

"Rob," Bianca scolded. "Jesus."

"It's okay." Noelle swallowed hard. "But I'm not alone. I have my children, and Emily, and another grandchild on the way." She smiled at Phoebe. "I have a busy life. I'm not lonely."

"Don't you miss being with someone, though?" Bianca whispered.

She couldn't think what to say to that.

"Well," Roberta said, "I think that if you were to—" She stopped short.

Noelle saw her staring toward the shop door. In some part of her mind she'd heard the bell over the door chime, but she hadn't registered that someone had come in.

She turned her head to see who it was, and inhaled sharply.

"Fuck," Roberta said.

Bianca and Phoebe glanced at her, frowning, then their eyes widened as they put two and two together. They looked back at the man standing in their shop, and their jaws sagged.

Noelle was struggling to breathe. Cameron wore a light-gray sweater over an open-necked white shirt, black jeans, and a gray jacket. He looked sophisticated and gorgeous, and she couldn't believe he was here, in Kerikeri, in her shop.

He glanced at her girls and his lips curved up a little. He walked forward slowly and stopped before them all, and his gaze settled on Noelle's.

"Hello," he said softly.

"Hey, Cameron," Roberta replied when it was clear her mother's brain was fried. "This is Bianca, and this is Phoebe, my sisters."

"Pleased to meet you." He shook their hands. "I'm so sorry to interrupt your afternoon, but I wondered whether I might have a quick chat with your mother."

"Of course." Roberta gestured toward the café. "Why don't you take a table in there and I'll make you both a coffee."

Cameron held up a hand for Noelle to precede him, so she led the way into the café and went over to a table and chairs by the window. Her best friend, Cathy, was serving behind the bar, and she shot her a quick glance, trying not to laugh at the sight of Cathy's wide eyes and opened mouth. She'd get grilled about this later. But first, she had to find out what he wanted.

"What can I get you?" Roberta asked Cameron.

"A latte would be great, thank you."

She nodded and left them to it.

Noelle didn't look at her daughters. Instead, her cheeks warm, she took a chair, and Cameron sat opposite her, leaning on the table.

Finally, she looked up at him and met his eyes.

"Hey," he said softly.

"Hey," she whispered back. "What are you doing here?"

"I had to see you again." His gaze caressed her face. "I couldn't leave it the way I did. I wanted to apologize."

"What for?"

"For saying you owed me. That was completely out of order, and I'm sorry."

She looked at her hands. "It's okay."

"It's not, and I really am sorry. I... was desperate, I guess. You were about to say no, and I'd had one too many whiskies, and I knew I'd never see you again. I panicked."

She adjusted the salt and pepper pots in the middle. "I couldn't, Cam."

"I know. It was probably wrong of me to ask, although I'm not sorry I did, and I don't regret that part of it. But I am sorry that it seemed as if I would have been happy with a one-night stand. Because that wasn't what it was about. I know what it must have looked like. I'd told you that I was divorced, and that I'd had affairs, and I was there on my own and you must have thought I wanted to take you back to my room as company for the night, before heading off the next day without a thought. And it wasn't like that at all."

"Cam—"

"I took one glance at you, Noelle, on the side of that dance floor, sipping your champagne and moving to the music, and I was lost. One glance. And when I walked out of that elevator, and I knew you were going to go back to your room and that would be it, I couldn't do it. I couldn't let you go again."

She lifted her gaze to his, speechless.

"Here you go." Roberta appeared at the table and placed their coffees in front of them, along with a plate of her mini muffins.

"Thank you." He smiled at her, and she grinned back before leaving them to it again.

"So that's your shop," he said, gesturing through the arch to the bridal shop as he popped a chocolate mini muffin in his mouth and chewed.

"It is," Noelle said, finally finding her voice. "The café is Roberta's."

"I like the archway. I would think it means customers can sit and have a drink while they ponder on their potential purchases."

"That's the plan. Plus we have fashion shows on Thursday nights, and we serve wine and nibbles here while a handful of us model the dresses. The evenings are quite popular now and people come from all over the Northland."

He smiled, his eyes returning to her. "You've done wonders."

She studied his face, feeling a mixture of elation and wistfulness. "How did you find me?"

"I flew to Kerikeri and asked for the bridal shop. There's only one."

"Oh, yes, I suppose so."

"I wasn't going to come." He looked down at his latte, at the beautiful silver fern that Roberta had traced in the foam on the top. "I was so angry with myself after you walked away, and I told myself that I didn't deserve to see you again. But early this morning, Rebecca—Marcus's wife—landed in Auckland, and we picked her up and had a coffee while we waited for our plane to Wellington. Marcus told her what had happened, and she said to me, 'So you let her go?' And I thought shit, yes I did, I'm such a fucking idiot. And that was it; I went to the flight desk and bought a charter flight, and here I am."

Her eyes nearly fell out of her head. "You bought a charter flight? Jesus, that must have been expensive."

"I don't know," he said honestly. "I didn't ask the price."

She blinked. "Cam… It is lovely to see you again, I can't deny that. But I don't know why you're here. You're just prolonging the inevitable. We live on opposite sides of the world, and nothing's going to change that."

He had a mouthful of his latte. "Maybe. But the thing is, I'm here, in New Zealand, until next weekend. I think I said, I have a meeting tomorrow in Wellington to discuss our bid for the Hokianga project. We've been invited to lunch with Te Papa Museum and the Maritime Archaeological Association—Rebecca's going with Marcus, and I thought… well, I wondered whether you would come with me."

She stared at him. "To the meeting?"

"Well, yes. I always think people seem more trustworthy if they're in a steady relationship, so you could be my… you know…"

She raised her eyebrows. "You want to hire me to be Mrs. Taylor for your meeting?"

"Well it didn't sound like that in my head. And anyway, I don't just mean that." He reached out and took her hand. "I mean for the week. Fly down to Wellington with me. Come to the meeting. Then we could do whatever you wanted; stay in Wellington, or I thought maybe we could drive back and visit a few places."

He lifted her hand to his lips and kissed her fingers. "I'm not expecting anything. I'll book us separate rooms. I just want to be with you. To spend some time with you. I'm not ready to let you go again, not yet. So I suppose the question is, do you want to spend some time with me?"

Chapter Seven

Noelle's head was spinning so fast she had no idea what to say.

Cameron was inviting her away for a dirty weekend. Actually, a dirty week. Except he'd said he'd book them separate rooms. He wasn't going to push her into a sexual relationship she wasn't ready for. But surely, if he was asking her to go away with him, he was going to expect something in return?

"You're suspicious," he said, reading her expression.

"It would be odd if I wasn't."

"Why's it so strange that I would want to spend some time with the woman I thought I'd lost forever?" He tipped his head to the side, a smile on his lips.

"It's not," she said slowly. "I suppose I'm questioning how sensible it would be to spend time together. We're going to have to part in the end. We're only prolonging the inevitable."

"Maybe. All I know is that I'm not ready to let you go. Perhaps I will be in a week, when we've had a chance to catch up properly. If I'm not... we'll have to talk about it then. I've learned not to look too far ahead. Right here, right now, I just want to be with you."

We'll have to talk about it then? What did he mean by that? Was he saying that somehow they could have a future together?

He was still holding her hand, and he brushed his thumb across her knuckles. "I want to spend time talking to you, and getting to know you again. To learn all about your life, with your kids and with Hugh. To find out if you still like Mexican food, and hate rhubarb."

That made her laugh. "I do."

"And I have to admit, I do have a bit of a motive for asking you. I know very little about New Zealand. I want to make a good impression at the meeting, and I'd be grateful if you'd tell me a bit about your country and its history so I don't look a complete idiot." He brushed her knuckles again. "We'd have an amazing time," he insisted. "I'll book us into the most exclusive hotel, and buy you exquisite food and the best wines in return. I'll spoil you rotten. Don't you think you deserve it?"

Ooh, that was tempting. But she wasn't going to admit that to him. "Don't try to bribe me," she teased instead.

A frown flickered on his brow. "I didn't mean it like that."

"I was joking, Cam."

"I meant what I said. I'll book separate rooms. There would be no pressure, I swear."

"So you wouldn't want to sleep with me?"

He gave her a wry look, obviously sensing she was still teasing him. "I'm not saying that. I can't think of anything I'd rather do than get naked with you again."

Her face burned immediately. It was a hot flash, she told herself. She wasn't blushing at the idea of stripping Cameron's clothes off.

"The hotel in Wellington has a sunken bath," he said. "Big enough for two."

"Oh Jesus."

He chuckled. "Come on, you teased me—I'm teasing you. Of course it would be wonderful if we reconnected like that. But I get your point. We're not twenty anymore. It's been three decades, and you've only been with your husband all that time. You're bound to be wary. And I swear to you that if we spend the whole week just talking and being together, I won't be disappointed."

The sting of tears made her blink. His eyes were kind—he meant every word. But it didn't change the fact that she would feel obligated. He would be hoping they'd sleep together, and she didn't know if she could, should, or wanted to.

Okay, maybe she wanted to, a little. But fantasizing about something and actually doing it were two different things, especially where sex was concerned.

"Can I think about it?" she whispered.

He nodded. "I have a plane booked for nine-thirty tomorrow morning."

"Would I get a ticket this late?"

He smiled. "It's a charter flight. The plane seats twelve, and there's only me at the moment."

Holy moly. A private plane all the way to Wellington.

She mustn't get distracted by the lure of fancy things. "I'll call you later, once I've had a chance to think about it."

"Of course. I was thinking, though, as I am up here, maybe you'd like to go to dinner later?"

"Oh. Um… sure."

He checked his watch. "It's four-thirty. Shall I pick you up at, say, seven?"

"Okay." She told him her address, and he programmed it and her number into his phone, which was, she noticed from the symbol on the back, a sleek Goldvish. She was sure she'd read an article that stated they cost a cool ten thousand dollars.

"All right." He pocketed his phone and rose. "I'll leave you to work. But I'll see you tonight."

She rose too and glanced over her shoulder. Cathy and Roberta were serving customers and doing their best not to look as if they were watching the scene unfolding at the table by the window. Bianca and Phoebe happened to be dressing a mannequin in the shop that also had a perfect view of them.

She looked back at Cameron, who gave her a mischievous smile. "Don't you think it would be nice to escape somewhere that people weren't watching your every move?"

"Go away, you wicked man."

He laughed, leaned forward, and pressed his lips to her cheek. Then he was gone, leaving behind the seductive smell of expensive aftershave and a hitch in her heartbeat that she knew would take a while to calm down.

"Oh. My. God." Roberta came over immediately, her sisters and Cathy hot on her heels. "What happened? What did he say?"

Noelle's hands were shaking. "He wants to… um… hire me, sort of, to help out at a business meeting he's going to, and teach him a bit about the country's history… in Wellington… for a week…"

"He wants to take you away." Bianca's face lit up with a smile. Roberta grinned. Phoebe glanced at her sisters, then gave her mother a hesitant smile.

"I haven't said yes yet," Noelle told them. "I said I needed to think about it. He wants to take me out to dinner tonight and I'll give him my answer then." She made a shooing motion with her hands. "Now leave me alone to finish my coffee. I need to think."

The girls walked off, talking in hushed whispers, as Noelle sank back into her chair.

Cathy perched opposite her. "You okay?"

"No."

"I can understand that. He's gorgeous! Why didn't you tell me how gorgeous he was?"

"I forgot," Noelle said.

Cathy gave her a pitying look. "This is a good thing. Isn't it? Isn't it an amazing thing?"

"I don't know." Noelle's brow furrowed, and she glanced over her shoulder at her daughters. "I feel so mixed up, Cath. I've walked away from him twice, and he's still come back for more. I'm incredibly flattered, but also so confused."

"What's confusing? He's hot, and you haven't had sex in over two years."

"That's what's scaring the shit out of me. If I go away with him, he's going to want sex."

"One can only hope."

"Cath!"

Her best friend rolled her eyes. "Only you could see that as a problem."

Noelle bit her lip as tears pricked her eyes. "Don't mock me."

Cathy's expression softened, and she took Noelle's hands in hers. "Aw, come on. I'm half teasing. How many times have we joked about backpacking to Europe and finding ourselves a toy-boy?"

It was a joke on Cathy's part; she'd been happily married for fifteen years, but the two women occasionally drank a few too many Cosmos and fantasized about escaping from their lives, which were both centered around their busy, demanding families.

"I know," Noelle whispered. "But it's one thing to daydream… It's another to actually do it. What about Hugh? What about my kids?"

"It looks as if they think it's a great idea," Cathy pointed out.

"The girls might say so, but I'm not sure about Phoebe, and she is pregnant…"

"She's also strong and a grown woman, and I know she wants you to be happy."

"Hugh was her father," Noelle said softly. "I don't want anyone to think I'm being disloyal or unfaithful."

Cathy's brow creased. "Sweetheart… You were lucky to find Hugh, and incredibly unlucky to lose him at the age of fifty. Nobody, but nobody, would expect you to stay single for the next twenty or thirty years. Your kids might feel funny about you seeing someone else because they loved their dad and it will remind them that he's gone, and that things change, and everyone hates change. But they're good kids. They wouldn't want you to be faithful to his memory at the expense of your own happiness."

"I know. I know I'm being silly."

"No, you're not being silly at all, you're going through exactly what I'd go through if I were in your position. But something tells me... is there another reason you're... not afraid, but... reticent to go?"

Noelle gave her a wry look. "You know perfectly well what the problem is. I'm fifty-two!"

"He must be older than you."

"Yes, but that's not the point. Men tend to age well. He still swims, he's kept fit..."

"You do Pilates," Cathy pointed out. "You get your hair and nails done. You eat well and look after yourself."

"Cathy! You know what I'm trying to say." She shot her friend a glare.

Cathy pursed her lips. "You're talking about getting naked."

"Of course I'm talking about getting naked! It's been two years since I've had sex, and that was with a man who'd watched me age over thirty years, and who knew and loved every bump and bulge and wrinkle on my body. The last time Cameron saw me naked, I was eighteen. I've changed a little bit since then."

"I know. I do know."

"When I think of some of the things we got up to... I couldn't get in half those positions now and still be able to walk in the morning."

Cathy chuckled. "It would be fun finding out, though, wouldn't it?"

"It terrifies me. He's divorced, and he's been hooking up with women in bars all his life, it sounds like. I would imagine they're young women, wouldn't you? This isn't like two old fogies meeting up at the retirement village and caressing each other's zimmer frames. He's like George Clooney or... or... Michael Douglas, or something, I'm sure he has women flocking around him, and I'm... me."

"Yes, and you're an intelligent, gorgeous woman in her prime—"

"Hardly."

"—with a successful business and, God willing, twenty or thirty years ahead of her to continue to make a difference in this world. You can spend the rest of your life babysitting your grandkids and helping everyone else get on with their lives, or you can do something amazing with your own. Doesn't that sound fun?"

"I don't do fun anymore." It wasn't true; of course it wasn't true. She had a great life. And if she spent the rest of it making sure she was there if her children needed her, and helping to raise her grandchildren, she'd be happy with that.

Or at least, she would have been. Ignorance is bliss and all that. She'd thought many times over the years about how different her life might have been if she'd stayed with Cameron. If she didn't go with him now, would she spend the next thirty years wishing she'd made a different decision?

"If I were to go," she said slowly, "I'd have to leave tomorrow morning. I don't suppose you'd be around to run the shop?"

"Of course!" Cathy looked delighted. "You know I love working in there. I'll absolutely do that for you." A customer approached the counter, and Cathy stood and gave her best friend a hug. "There are always a thousand reasons not to do something. And you don't have to, darling, not if you're really worried about it. Follow your heart, my love. You won't go far wrong there."

Noelle hugged her back, then watched her return to work before turning her attention to the view of the street outside the window.

Follow her heart… If only it were that easy.

While she finished off her coffee, she took out her phone and texted Dominic, asking if she could call in after work. He texted back immediately that he'd be home by six, and he'd see her then.

She'd just put the phone down when Elliot came into the shop. He wore his navy-blue police officer's uniform, although he wasn't wearing his peaked cap.

"Hey you," she said, accepting his hug. "How are you doing?"

"Good," he said, because like any man he would never give a long answer when a short one would do. She eyed him critically as he took the seat opposite hers. After breaking up with his long-term girlfriend the month before, Elliot had found himself a small house in the center of Kerikeri and was now living on his own. Despite Noelle's attempts to teach him to cook as he'd grown up, he'd never mastered anything beyond the basics of heating up a tin of baked beans, and as a result she could see that he'd lost weight.

"You need fattening up," she said.

"I'm here to talk about you, not about my waistline." He looked around the café. "Is he here?"

She realized one of his sisters must have texted him to say what was happening. "Cameron? No, he left. Why? Were you going to ask him what his prospects are?"

His lips curved up. "No… I wanted to meet the man who's got my mother in a tizz."

Her face warmed. "I'm not in a tizz."

"Roberta said you were."

"Well, Roberta can go and… mind her own business."

"Mum…" His expression softened. "Rob said he's asked you to go away with him."

Noelle dropped her gaze to her empty cup and played with the spoon.

"Why wouldn't you?" he asked. "Don't you think it would be fun?"

"I don't know."

"Are you worried what everyone's going to think?"

She gave a little shrug. "That's partly it."

"Well the point is that even if we didn't agree—and we do, all of us—it's your life, Mum."

"I know."

"It's not like Dad died a month ago," he said gently. "Or even a year ago. You've been on your own a long time. You spend pretty much your whole life looking after other people. I think you deserve some fun and happiness."

Tears pricked her eyes. "Everyone's making me cry today."

"Aw. I don't mean to. Look, I've got to go but I wanted to call in and say that I know you don't need my approval, but for what it's worth, you have it, and I think you should go."

She bit her lip hard. "That means a lot, Elliot. Thank you."

"All right. Let me know if there's anything I can do." He stood and kissed the top of her head, then picked up a takeaway coffee from his sister before heading out of the door.

Noelle went back into the bridal shop. A group of young women were checking out the rack of gowns, giggling amongst themselves, and she knew at least one of them would probably be trying the dresses on soon. Not long and then she'd go and see Dominic. And maybe after that, she'd finally be able to make up her mind what she was going to say to Cameron.

SERENITY WOODS

Chapter Eight

At six o'clock, Noelle rang the bell at Dominic's house.

His daughter, Emily, answered the door, and immediately threw her arms around her grandmother's waist. "Nanna!"

"Hello sweetheart." Noelle hugged her, not missing the pang of guilt that poked her in the stomach like a broom handle. She was a grandmother, and she was thinking about having a dirty week away! Shocking!

"Come in. Fliss is making brownies and I'm helping."

"So I see." Noelle smiled at the smudge of chocolate on her granddaughter's cheek and followed her inside. "It's only me," she called, going through to the kitchen.

"Hello!" Fliss turned from her baking to give her mother-in-law a kiss. She wore her blonde hair pinned up, and her beautiful face glowed from the heat of the oven. "Lovely to see you. How are you?"

"Good, thank you. I see you're busy baking."

"Emily has a few friends coming around tonight for a sleepover, so we're getting ready with some midnight snacks." Fliss pulled a face, then smiled. It wasn't the first time she'd had the girls over, and Dominic had told his mother that she'd enjoyed every minute of it. Clearly she didn't seem to miss her old life as an actress very much.

"We're going to sleep in the living room with sleeping bags," Emily said. "Dad's making us a tent out of blankets and Fliss has bought some of those battery candles so it looks as if we're around a campfire."

"Too cold to have a real camping excursion in the garden," Fliss said.

"Fair enough." Noelle kissed her granddaughter's hair. "I hope you have a lovely time."

"Dominic's in his study," Fliss told her. "Go on through; he's expecting you. Do you want a coffee?"

"No thank you, just had one." Noelle gave her a smile, then went along the corridor to Dominic's study at the back of the house. The room was simply decorated with an oak desk and chair facing the window that looked out onto the garden, a comfy armchair where he sat and read, and several shelves full of books. Her son turned as she entered and rose to give her a hug and a kiss on the temple.

"Hey." He squeezed her before releasing her, and gestured for her to take the armchair. "That was a surprise text today. Everything okay?"

"Yes, yes. Fine." Noelle perched on the edge and studied her handsome son. A deacon at the local church, Dominic had lost his first wife several years ago, but had been lucky enough to find love again with Fliss. He'd chosen not to become a priest but remained a deacon, helping out in the local community alongside his job as a counsellor at the town's high school. He was a good man, and Noelle was immensely proud of him.

She cleared her throat. "Have any of the girls messaged you today?"

"No. Should they have?"

"No, no. I just wondered."

"Mum." Dominic frowned. "What's going on?"

Noelle glanced at the door, then rose to push it shut before taking her seat again. "I wanted to talk about Jo," she said softly.

Dominic's green eyes, so similar to all her children, studied her thoughtfully. "Okay."

"I hope you don't mind."

"Of course not."

"You rang me one night, when you'd met Fliss. You had questions... about dating again."

He leaned back in his chair, linked his fingers, and rested an ankle on his other knee. "I remember."

"You said you were worried about being haunted by your memories. I just wondered... do you find that? I don't want you to feel disloyal to Fliss, but... I felt the need to talk about it."

He looked at his hands for a moment, thinking. Then he raised his gaze to her again. "Sometimes I wonder whether Jo is out there, somewhere, watching me. Whether she's angry, or upset, because I found love with someone else. But I think that's the man in me talking, the ego, if you will. I don't think we carry negative feelings with us to Heaven. And I don't think the love we have is limited. It's not like we're given ten liters of it to use up by the time we die, and if we use it all on one person, we have none left if they die before us. For me, the love God gives us is a renewable resource; it's like solar energy— the sun keeps on shining every day, and we can absorb as much of it as we want and let it shine onto everyone we meet."

"That's a beautiful way to think of it."

He shrugged and smiled. "You told me that you can't be unfaithful to someone who's passed away."

"Me and my big mouth."

He chuckled. Then he gave her an appraising look. "You also said that if you had the chance to love and be loved by another man, you wouldn't be able to walk away from that." His eyes surveyed her, warm and gentle. "Who is he?"

Her face heated. "Do you remember me telling you about Cameron Taylor?"

"Your first boyfriend in England? Of course."

"I met him at the ball in Auckland. Out of the blue. You could have knocked me down with a feather. And I'm sure there are many other clichés to explain how I felt, but they've all gone right out of my head."

"Wow. It must have been a shock."

"It was."

"So…"

"He's asked me to go away with him for a week. He has an important business meeting in Wellington, and he said it would be nice for him to have a companion for it as his colleague's wife has flown over here and he doesn't want to feel like a fifth wheel, so he's going to sort of mock-hire me to go with him. He said he'd book separate rooms." Her face burned hotter.

Dominic didn't laugh or tease her, though. He leaned forward, elbows on his knees, and smiled at her. "It sounds like the perfect opportunity to spend some time with an old friend."

A sudden rush of emotion tightened her throat and made tears prick her eyes. "You're such a nice man."

He tipped his head to the side. "Do you want my permission? Is that why you came? Either as your son or… spiritually?"

"No… I know I don't need anyone's permission, not really."

"Well you know you have it. Of course you have it. You made Dad so happy. But you've been alone nearly two years, and as you told me,

I don't think God would think badly of you for finding comfort with someone else."

"Thank you. It means a lot to me."

"What did the others say?"

"Elliot told me to go for it. The girls were supportive… mostly."

He raised his eyebrows.

"I'm worried about Phoebe," she said. "With the baby. She didn't say anything, but she took your father's death so hard, and I don't want to upset her by making her think I've forgotten about him, and don't love him anymore."

"Phoebe's not dumb, Mum. She might feel a bit weird about it, but she wouldn't think you'd stopped loving Dad." He smiled. "What else?"

Noelle's lips parted as she went to deny it, and then she gave him a rueful smile. "It's weird to talk about it with my son."

"Yeah, I get it. But I've been there. Dating again after so long is scary. When you've been with a person a long time, you don't see their spare tires or wrinkles or stretch marks. All I can say is that if you were going to date a twenty-year-old, I'd think you had a point, but if he's the same age as you, even if he's kept fit, he's going to be having the same concerns."

"I'm not so sure… I didn't think men worried about that kind of thing."

"He was crazy about you, and he hasn't seen you for thirty years. Believe me, it's going to be on his mind."

"I'm not saying I'm going to… you know…"

He got up and pulled her to her feet, then wrapped his arms around her. "You don't have to explain yourself to me, or to anyone, in fact. Go with him, Mum. Get to know him again, have some fun. You've earned it."

She rested her cheek on his chest, finding comfort in the warmth of his arms. She missed this—being hugged by someone, being loved. All her children were affectionate, but exchanging pecks on the cheek was so different from being physically close like this.

"I'm worried I'll fall for him again," she whispered. "He's only here a week. And he runs a huge business based in London, and he flies all over the world. He's not going to want to come and live here in New Zealand."

"You could always go to England."

"I couldn't, Dom. My life is here. I couldn't leave you all, especially with Phoebe being pregnant, and I know the rest of you aren't going to be far behind."

"Has Dr. Angus been talking?"

She moved back and her eyes widened. "Oh, Dom…"

He smiled. "Fliss has only just found out, so we're keeping it quiet. Don't say anything because we don't want to tell Emily yet. But I wanted you to know."

Noelle threw her arms around his neck and hugged him tightly. "I'm so, so pleased for you."

"Thank you. We're both thrilled, and I know Emily's going to be excited when we tell her."

"Your and Phoebe's babies will be roughly the same age. That's going to be such a help for both her and Fliss. And the kids will be able to play together!"

"The perfect storm."

She brought his hands up and kissed his fingers. It was wonderful news, although it cemented her feelings that this was where she was needed, and where she belonged. She'd never push herself on her children, but mothers of newborns always needed extra help even if they didn't think they did, and she would hate not to be there if they needed her.

"But you mustn't let it influence your decision," Dominic scolded. "There are always a thousand reasons not to do something."

A shiver went down Noelle's back. "Cathy told me the exact same thing."

"There you go. It's true. Go away with him, Mum. Have the time of your life for a week and worry about the future later. Love will find a way; it always does, no matter what we have planned."

She glanced at the clock on his wall. It was nearly six-thirty, and she had to go home and get changed. "I'd better go. He's picking me up for dinner at seven. But thank you for talking to me. You always make me feel better."

"I'm glad I could help. When would you be flying out?"

"Tomorrow morning." She gave him an impish look. "On a charter flight."

"Oh… I see." He grinned. "Then you've definitely got to go."

"I didn't think deacons placed such importance on money."

"They don't. But as you're fond of telling me, I'm only human, and you deserve to be spoiled. Now go on. I've got thirty minutes to make a tent out of blankets."

Noelle said goodbye to Fliss and an excited Emily, then got into her car and drove back to her house.

As she changed, she thought about Dominic's news, smiling at the notion of being a grandmother again. Roberta and Angus were due to get married in the New Year, and she doubted that Bianca and Freddie would wait longer than a couple of months before naming the day, so more grandchildren were certainly on the way. There was only Elliot to sort out, and then all her kids would be happily married.

She pulled on a light-blue sweater over a white shirt, combined it with navy slacks, and then put on a little mascara and lipstick while she thought about her younger son. Elliot had feelings for Libby Carter; that much had been obvious to her for a long time. If Libby hadn't lost her partner in the plane crash back in July, Noelle thought that she and Elliot might have been a couple by now. But Libby's loss meant that Elliot would have to wait until she was ready to move on, and who knew when that would be? It had only been four months since the crash; Noelle had been single for nearly two years, and she was still worried that people would think she was moving too fast.

Her hand paused in the process of putting on her lipstick, and she studied her reflection and pressed her lips together. It wasn't too quick. She knew it wasn't, and that her fear of what people might think wasn't the real problem. She was scared of loving again, and especially scared of losing Cameron a second time.

But she wasn't going to let fear rule her. Tonight she'd tell him that she would go with him, and she'd stay in her own room, and they'd have to see how things went. If it didn't feel right, she wasn't going to sleep with him. She didn't want to sully her memories of Hugh with a meaningless one-night stand she'd end up regretting in the cold light of day.

A car scrunched on the gravel of the drive, and her pulse sped up a little. She went to walk out of the bedroom, then paused in the doorway and backed up a few steps to the chest of drawers that stood against the wall. On the top was a selection of photographs in various frames, one of each of her children with their partners, and one of her granddaughter. At the end of the row, Hugh smiled at her out of a frame he'd bought her for their thirtieth wedding anniversary, just a month before he died. She'd assumed they'd make it to their Ruby wedding, and she'd been thinking about planning a cruise for it around Asia. If there was any lesson she should take away from Hugh's death, it was never to plan too far ahead, and always to live for today.

She studied her left hand for a moment. Slowly, she slid the plain gold band off her third finger. She kissed it and placed it in front of Hugh's photo.

Then she left the room.

Chapter Nine

Cameron had hired a car at the Bay of Islands airport when he'd arrived, and he pulled up outside Noelle's house just before seven. After turning off the engine, he got out of the car and looked around as he walked up to the front door.

The large house sat in front of an enormous lawn overlooking the Waitangi Forest, with mandarin trees on one side and a kiwifruit orchard on the other. He could see a pool behind the house. That surprised him. He owned a pool because it was important for him to stay fit and confident in the water, but he was very unusual. In England you had to be rich to possess one, or to have a decent-sized garden for that matter. Available land was in short supply in the UK, but from what he'd seen in the windows of the real estate agent in town, here it seemed common to have several acres, and many houses had pools.

He stood out the front, suddenly nervous about ringing the bell. This was the house Noelle had shared with her late husband. Hugh had come home here after work every evening, probably parked his car in the spot where Cameron's was now, and gone inside to give his wife a kiss. She'd been happily married to this man for thirty years.

Cameron felt a twist of envy, and an overriding sense of sadness at the thought that it could have been him.

Lifting a hand, he rang the bell. Only seconds later the door opened. "Hello!" Noelle smiled at him. "Right on time."

"Wouldn't want to keep a lovely lady waiting." His gaze skimmed down her as she turned to fetch her coat and purse. She looked slender and elegant in her slacks and sweater, and she pulled on a smart black coat.

"Are you all right?" she asked as she came out and shut the door behind her. "You've got a weird look on your face."

"It's my regular face, but thank you for noticing."

She nudged him as they walked to the car. "Are you sure? You haven't changed your mind?"

"No, of course not, nothing like that." He walked around to the passenger side of the car and stopped with his hand on the door handle. "I'm nervous."

Her eyebrows rose. "Nervous about what my answer will be?"

"No. Well, yes. But I mean I'm nervous about this." He gestured at the two of them. "Dating again."

She studied his face, and smiled slowly. "Really?"

"I haven't dated properly since… hmm… the last time we dated." He opened the door.

She frowned at him before sliding into the seat. "You must have dated your ex-wife though?"

He closed the door, walked around the car, and got in the driver's side. After starting the engine and heading toward the road, he finally answered her. "Not really. In the beginning we went straight from bar to bed, and after that we were always in a rush, as both our businesses were growing. We never seemed to spend time together the way you and I did." His memories were filled with those days; walking on the South Bank in the summer, on their way to a performance at the Olivier; lying in Regent's Park, his head in Noelle's lap, as he read to her from a battered copy of *To Kill a Mockingbird*; curled up around each other in bed on a Sunday morning as rain hammered against the window, spending hours kissing and touching each other.

"That's sad," she said.

"It is." He paused at the junction with the main road then turned toward the town center.

"Well, look, I wanted to say now rather than make you wait all evening. If the offer's still there, I'd like to go to Wellington with you."

He stared at her for a long moment, pleasure filling him. "Really?"

"Really." She smiled. "But, if it's okay, I'd like to have my own room. I'm happy to pay for it."

"I wouldn't dream of it, and of course you can. As I said, I'll be thrilled to have you there."

To his surprise, he meant it. This was completely different from hooking up with a one-night stand in a bar. This was about getting to know the woman he'd loved and lost, and he was elated that she'd agreed to come.

"Where are we going?" she asked, looking out of the window.

"I booked us a table at what looked like a nice restaurant on the inlet. The Partridge?"

"Oh yes, it's lovely there."

"Great." He passed the bridal shop and headed through the town.

"What have you been doing this afternoon?" she asked.

"I went out to Rainbow Falls, which was stunning."

"Did you stop yourself from diving in?"

He grinned. "I was tempted. There were kids jumping into the river right from the top of the waterfall. I'd have done that if I were ten years younger."

"I've done it," she said.

He laughed. "Why doesn't that surprise me?"

"I was only about twenty-two," she admitted. "It was after Dominic was born. I don't know why I did it. Maybe to prove I wasn't just a mum, you know? That I was still me." She looked out of the window.

He glanced at her, then returned his gaze to the road. Outwardly she'd changed a lot from the young girl he'd known. Inwardly, maybe not so much.

"What made you come to Kerikeri?" he asked, taking the road out of town toward the inlet.

She told him about how Hugh had bought a business in Whangarei, an hour's drive south, and then after a couple of years they'd moved again even further north.

"You're a long way from Auckland," he said, slowing the car and following the winding road down, past thick palms and ferns on either side. "Is that a problem for your bridal business?"

"No, not really. It's about the same distance as London to Plymouth, I guess. The Bay of Islands has its own little economy in many ways. Paihia and Russell are as big as Kerikeri, and the surrounding towns are slowly growing. It gets very busy here in the summer months. And we go to Auckland every other month or so, and keep in touch with the big businesses down there."

He turned the corner, remembering earlier that day when he'd driven there and been surprised as the view widened out and there was the inlet spread out before them. "It's lovely down here," he said, pulling the car into the car park of The Partridge hotel and restaurant.

"It was the first place in New Zealand to be settled by Pakeha," Noelle said, releasing her seat belt as he turned off the engine.

"Sorry, packy…"

"Pa-ke-ha. Europeans."

"Ah, yes, I've seen that written down. I wondered what it meant."

They closed the doors. "Come here," she said, taking his hand. She led him away from the restaurant and along the path. The road ended in a wide turning circle, fronted by a boarded pier with seats overlooking the river.

"This river basin is also known as the Kerikeri Mission Station," she said. "It was established in 1819. That's Kemp House or the Mission House." She gestured at a white-boarded building to the right. "It was completed in 1822, so it's the country's oldest building." She turned and indicated the large stone building to its left. "That's the Stone Store—the oldest stone building in the country, erected after about 1832. I thought it was really funny when I came here that it's relatively new! When you think how old the Tower of London is…"

"I get your point."

"There's a sad story about the Bean family, missionaries who helped build the Mission Station. Their three-year-old son, William, died here from some stomach problem. He was the first Pakeha to die and be buried in Kerikeri. That must have been very hard for them, to come all that way, three months of sailing, with all that hope of a new life, only to lose their boy. I used to come here and think about them when I had Dominic."

She was painting a picture of her early years here as somewhat wistful while she struggled to come to terms with being newly married and a mother in a new country. It must have been hard for her, he thought.

She walked forward a little. "When I first came here there was no bypass, and the original road crossed the inlet over a bridge." She gestured to where the river now tumbled across a layer of rocks. "But in 2007 we were hit by a huge storm. Two months of rain fell in twenty-four hours, and a tree was caught across the legs of the bridge. The river broke its banks and spilled right up to the steps of the Stone Store. It came very close to flooding and everyone was terrified we'd lose our oldest buildings. So after that they built the bypass and demolished the bridge."

Her eyes were distant, obviously remembering that day. He thought about how Hugh would have rung her to check on their children, and how they would have pulled together to make sure their house and family were safe.

"And up there is St. James Church." She pointed up the hill to a building made from white weatherboard with a red roof. "It was built around the same time as the other buildings. That's where Dominic works. It's a beautiful church. Maybe he'll show you around one day. And lastly, there's the wishing well. I've cast a few coins in there over the years." A touch of pink appeared in her cheeks. "One day, a long time ago, when I was feeling down, I wished that I'd see you again before I died. It took a long time to come true, but it did in the end."

He supposed it should make him feel good to think that she'd missed him over the years, but it didn't, it just made him sad.

She glanced up at him and smiled. "History lesson done. Come on."

He let her lead him up to The Partridge, and they went inside. To their right was a large bar with an open fire at one end. The restaurant itself was spacious, with glass sliding doors that were open to show a huge wooden deck, where more tables overlooked the river below. Round tables with white cloths and shining silver cutlery graced the room, about half of them with diners. Paintings of the Twelve Days of Christmas filled the walls. He'd fallen in love with the place when he'd stopped there for a coffee that afternoon, and had immediately booked a table for the evening.

"Good evening." A smiling Maori woman, her gray curls tipped with an interesting bright pink, approached them. "Noelle, how lovely to see you." The two women kissed on the cheek. "And Cameron, I didn't realize it was Noelle you were entertaining."

Impressed that she'd remembered his name, he smiled. "We're old friends, catching up." Her name was Aroha, he recalled, not pronounced like the Hawaiian *aloha* as he'd thought but with the same emphasis on all three syllables—*ah-roh-ha*. She'd told him earlier that it meant 'love' and had laughed, and he'd liked her immediately.

"How lovely." Even though she shot Noelle a curious look of *You'd better fill me in later*, Aroha didn't press for more details but gestured toward the corner of the room, where a table for two sat in a secluded spot—the best table in the house, as he'd requested.

They took their seats, and she handed them both a menu. "Can I get you a drink?"

He looked at Noelle. "White wine?"

"Please."

He checked the wine list and ordered a bottle of Sauvignon by the Blue Penguin Bay vineyard, which was expensive and therefore promised to be good. Aroha nodded and went off to get it, leaving them to peruse the menu.

"A friend of yours?" he said, running his gaze down the list of tempting dishes.

She laughed. "Yes. We met at our Pilates class and hit it off immediately. She's only recently taken over the place. Outside there's a pear tree which was planted by the first missionaries. That's why this is the Partridge, get it? The Partridge and the pear tree?"

"Oh, and hence all the paintings." He gestured at the one nearest them, which was of seven swans swimming in a huge lake.

"It's a great idea. She commissioned those paintings by an Auckland artist called Matt King—he's famous for the Ward Seven children's stories, don't know if you've come across them, but sometimes he does other artwork and she thought he'd be a good fit…" She continued talking about the paintings and how she and Aroha had sat down with the artist to talk about ideas.

Cameron was listening, but he found himself captivated by the moment, his attention drawn to the woman sitting before him. The sun was setting, turning Noelle's silver hair red and touching the tips of her eyelashes with gold. He couldn't believe that, after all this time, and all those years of wistful dreams, he was finally sitting here with her, talking as if no time had passed at all.

She met his gaze, and something passed between them, quick, sharp, and bright, like the flare of a firework. Her words died away, and her lips parted as she inhaled, obviously feeling it too.

"I've missed you," he said.

She swallowed. "I missed you too. I don't want you to think that leaving was easy for me. I'd made my bed, and I knew I had to lie in it. It was my choice, I knew that. It was the right choice, and I would make the same decision if I had my time again. I stayed with my parents, and I loved my husband and children. But that doesn't mean those first few years weren't hard. Very hard. I don't think you'll ever know how much I yearned for you."

He felt a strange sense of peace settle over him. She wasn't saying she'd made the wrong decision. He'd thought that would hurt more, but oddly it didn't. The years that had passed weren't wasted. Their paths had separated, and her life had been fulfilling. And so had his, he couldn't deny it. Maybe his marriage hadn't been perfect, but he'd had three healthy children, and his business had been his world.

But now their paths had crossed again, who knew what the future held?

She looked at her left hand and flexed it. "I was thinking tonight how important it is to live for today. There were things I should have done with Hugh that I didn't get around to, and that makes me sad. And I don't want to make the same mistake with you. I don't want to live with regret for the rest of my life."

He took her hand, brushing his thumb over the space where her wedding band had been. The removal of it was symbolic, he thought, a gesture that told him she was placing her life with Hugh to one side for a while.

"Me neither," he murmured.

She leaned forward on the table, and he did the same, bringing their lips together in a brief, soft kiss.

"So," Aroha said brightly, mischievously, appearing by their side. "What can I get you for dinner this evening?"

Chapter Ten

They had a long, slow meal, taking their time over each course as they talked about the intervening years. Noelle thought that Cam looked much more relaxed now he knew she was going with him to Wellington. The tension went from his shoulders, and he smiled much more often, something she was beginning to wonder whether he normally did on a daily basis.

They finished their meal with a portion each of one of the special ice creams that Aroha bought in from the *Treats to Tempt You* shop in Doubtless Bay. Noelle scraped her spoon around the glass dish, making sure she'd collected every last mouthful of the raspberry cream, pondering on what he'd been telling her about his company. It didn't sound as if he had much time for fun. "You've turned into a very serious man," she said.

"Life is serious," he said, doing the same with his dish of ginger cookie ice cream. "I'm busy, and when there's a lot of work to do we don't mess around much."

She didn't say anything, but she thought about her days, how she would listen to the chatter and giggle of young women as they tried on wedding gowns, and then she'd talk to her daughters, who were always smiling and making jokes. In the evenings she'd go out with Cathy or Aroha or some other friends, and although sometimes they talked about problems with their families or businesses, laughter was never far from the surface.

"You didn't used to be serious." She pushed away her dish. "Do you remember the night we went to The Lyceum?"

Cameron grinned and licked his spoon. "I do. We had sex in the public toilets during the interval, forgot to lock the door, and nearly gave an old woman a heart attack. We laughed all the way home."

"Those were the days." She smiled.

"Can I get you some coffee?" Aroha asked, approaching the table.

"Latte for me please," Noelle said, and Cameron nodded for the same. Aroha retreated to fetch it, taking their empty dishes with her.

Cameron turned his wine glass in his fingers. "You must have stories like that about Hugh."

Noelle gave him a wry look. "Don't fish for information. I feel uncomfortable talking to you about him."

"Why?"

"I don't know. I feel disloyal to him and to you." Her thoughts and feelings felt muddled. It reminded her of when the girls used to play with Plasticine, and they'd mix a ball of all the different colors together thinking it would come out like a rainbow, but it only ever turned a dirty gray-brown.

She stared at her wine glass. She shouldn't drink any more.

"You're not disloyal to either of us," he said. "I never thought you'd stay single in New Zealand. You're far too gorgeous for that. I don't feel hurt that you met and married Hugh. A tad envious, maybe, that he got to spend all those years with you, but I don't resent him for it. He sounds like a great guy. Maybe we'd have been friends if we'd have met."

She gave him an uncertain smile. She was sure he wouldn't have liked the solid, unflappable Hugh. He'd been a great father, a faithful husband, and a good friend, but, if she were honest, he hadn't been the most exciting man on the planet. He'd seemed to enjoy his job in construction but hadn't had any real passion about it; it had been a way to pay the bills and that was about it. He'd enjoyed gardening, and because they'd had that in common they'd spent a lot of time looking around garden centers, reading about plants and flowers, buying things for the garden, and working out there. He'd had some interest in World War II and had owned a few books he'd kept in his Man Cave—as the girls had named it—which he'd read while sitting out there with a cup of tea and a piece of cake. He'd sometimes made models of the planes he'd read about, and he'd painted them meticulously, then suspended them from the roof of the shed on bits of twine. They were still there; she hadn't had the heart to take them down.

But that was about it. He'd watched the All Blacks play rugby because she and the kids had always wanted to see it, but he hadn't been into sport. He'd never had any interest in cooking. He'd sometimes liked listening to country music, but again, he hadn't been passionate about it. He hadn't been passionate about anything much.

Not even her. She didn't think it reflected how he'd felt about her; it just hadn't been in his nature. He'd never been jealous or angry with her. He'd courted her gently, almost as if he hadn't expected her to say yes to going out with him, and when she had, their relationship had progressed the same way, gentle and slow. When they'd finally gotten to bed, his lovemaking had been tender and considerate, good enough that it had never been a problem, but somewhat predictable, eventually evolving into a once-a-fortnight exercise, and he'd always seemed rather relieved when it was over. The one and only time she'd suggested something even vaguely kinky—asking him whether he thought tying her up would be fun—he'd looked at her with surprise and something akin to horror. Embarrassed, she hadn't mentioned it again.

Hugh had liked everyone, so she knew he would have been pleasant to Cameron, but she couldn't imagine they'd have had anything in common. Hugh wouldn't have understood Cam's passion about archaeology, or his relationship with his wife and his affairs. But he'd have been too polite to say anything, and would simply have turned away to concentrate on his small life and his small thoughts.

Her face flushed. What a terrible thing to think. He was her husband, and he'd died. She put her face in her hands. Jesus Christ. What was she doing?

"Noelle?" Cameron leaned on the table, his voice full of concern. "What's the matter?"

"I'm such an awful wife."

"I'm sure that's not true." Now his voice held a smile.

She lowered her hands, blinking back tears. "I am."

"Why? Were you unfaithful to Hugh?"

"Of course not."

"Did you put him down in front of your friends or his friends?"

"No."

"Did you belittle him to his face?"

"You know that's not what I mean."

"Then what?"

She leaned her elbows on the table and rested her lips on her fingers. "I can't help but compare him to you, and that makes me feel bad."

Cameron went to reply, then stopped and smiled as Aroha returned with the coffees. When she'd retreated, he admired the fern shape she'd drawn on the top before taking a mouthful. Then he surveyed Noelle with a smile. "Sweetheart, I would think it's perfectly natural to compare. And it doesn't mean you're disloyal or mean to either of us. I'm sure he was a better man than me in many ways. I have a million faults! I'm impatient, sarcastic, irritable in the morning, I have no time for idiots, and I say what I think and most people don't like that. I'm obsessive about my work and dismissive of those who don't understand it. I'm not very good at compromising, although Marcus has helped me work on that. I can be snobbish, which I don't like, and again, I'm working on that. And I'm sure Hugh was the same. He'd have had good points and not-so-good points. We all do. All you're doing is recognizing them, that's all. That's not being disloyal. He wasn't an angel, and neither am I. As soon as we both accept that, I think we're going to be fine."

She took a big mouthful of her coffee, enjoying the flavor of burnt toffee and letting the heat of it comfort her. "I am sorry. I'm sure this is the last thing you wanted to talk about when you asked me to go with you."

"It's exactly what I wanted to talk about. That, and everything else." He laid a hand on the table, palm up, and she placed hers into it. His fingers curled around hers. "Life's not black and white," he told her. "Not right or wrong. It's all shades of gray. I know that over the next week I'll do or say things that will make you think Hugh wouldn't have done that. That's okay. I'm not expecting to replace your husband of thirty years. Again, once you get your head around that, I'm sure you'll feel better."

It was a lovely thing for him to say, but she knew he didn't quite understand.

Living with Hugh had been like sitting in front of a real fire late at night, when the logs glowed, filling the house with a pleasant warmth so that she never noticed how cold it was outside. Occasionally, when she poked the fire, the flames would dance for a while in the grate, but they soon died away, leaving only embers.

Being with Cameron had been like living in a blacksmith's furnace that was constantly fanned with bellows. She'd been afraid she might lose her eyebrows half the time. Everything about him had been turned up to eleven: his delight in food, music, history, sport… He'd had an opinion on everything, and he'd spoken passionately about any topic brought up in a conversation. He'd had a fierce temper, but a second later it was gone, and then he'd wanted to make up in a way that had left her breathless for days.

Hugh had been a sweetheart, and she'd been happy with him, but he couldn't compare to the man sitting before her, and for some reason that made her want to cry.

"I think I'm ready to go home," she said, finishing off her coffee and collecting her coat.

Cameron didn't say anything. He paid the bill and they waved goodbye to Aroha and went out into the cool evening.

He stopped as they passed the wishing well, took out a gold coin, and tossed it in. She looked at him, waiting for him to say something, but he just walked to the car, so she followed him, knowing anyway what he'd wished for, her stomach churning.

"Have you changed your mind?" he asked as he put the car in Drive and pulled away. "About coming to Wellington with me?"

"No," she said. "I suppose I need time to think about things. To adjust to being with you again. You're very... different. You make me feel eighteen again. And I don't quite know how to feel about that."

"Is it a bad thing?" He headed up the hill toward the town. His handsome face was in shadow.

"No," she said softly. "You make me feel... alive."

He glanced at her, then back at the road, and they didn't say anything else until he made the turn into town.

She pointed out a few sites: the clocktower, the library in the shape of the prow of a ship, the little cinema with its adjoining café.

"It's a lovely place," Cameron said, heading out of town down Inlet Road, into the darkness as the street lamps ran out.

"It is. I wish you could spend more time here; I think you'd like it."

He didn't reply, and she gave a silent sigh as he turned onto her drive and headed down to the house. There was no point in wishing they had more time. She had a week, and she'd have to make the most of the days they had.

He drew up in front of the house, put the handbrake on, then turned in the seat to look at her.

"I hope you don't mind if I don't ask you in," she said. "It's just... it's Hugh's house, and it wouldn't feel right..."

"I've left the engine running," he pointed out. "I wasn't expecting you to." He smiled. "Thank you for a lovely evening."

She unbuckled her seat belt. "Thank you. It was a gorgeous meal and I had a really nice time."

"I'm glad."

She hesitated. 'Really nice' didn't cover it at all. He'd been entertaining, amusing, and fun. She hadn't enjoyed herself so much for years.

Either she was going to do this or she wasn't. She had to make the choice now, because it wasn't fair on Cameron to pretend they were mere acquaintances when they had been—and might still be—much more than that.

She'd heard of the theory of parallel universes, where all the choices a person could make were played out in alternate realities. It was up to her which one she picked.

She could tell him right now that she'd changed her mind, leave the car, and never see him again. Was that what she wanted? Or was that guilt and fear talking?

She didn't want to be the sort of person who was too afraid to take risks. She'd much rather regret doing something than not doing it.

"Cam," she whispered. "Can I kiss you goodnight?"

He grinned then, a smile filled with pleasure and delight. "You have to ask?" He unbuckled his belt and pulled her into his arms.

She laughed and lifted a hand to his face, feeling the line of his jaw and the slight hint of stubble beneath her fingers. The moon was half full, so there was a little light, casting him in silver, and she inhaled at the glitter of his eyes.

He lowered his head, and she closed her eyes and accepted his kiss.

His mouth was warm, firm. He tilted his head to the side, changing the angle of the kiss, slanting his lips across hers, and she felt the brush of his tongue on her bottom lip. Her heart leapt. There was no tentative touch of the lips, no butterfly presses of his mouth against hers. Just full-on heat. Somehow he'd slipped his hand beneath her coat, and although it only rested in the small of her back, it was a small, thrilling invasion of the privacy that had been enforced on her for the last two years. His other arm was around her shoulders, holding her tightly against him the way he always had, possessive and demanding. He was explaining how he felt right from the start, telling her that he didn't consider them strangers and that he was going to claim what he felt was rightfully his.

The years melted away, and she was eighteen again, excited and turned on by his passion, his forcefulness. Her heart beat a rapid tattoo on her ribs, and she slid her hand into his hair and clenched her fingers, straining for the kiss, glad in a way not to have to pretend that she didn't want this, to play around with polite, respectable pecks. She didn't want to be grandmother-Noelle, or bridal-shop-Noelle, or anyone except the woman who still had desires and needs she was convinced this man could fulfil.

Her tongue slid against his, and she heard him give an approving murmur deep in his throat, a sound so sexy and guttural that her nipples tightened in her bra and she felt an answering clench deep inside. His hand was warm at the base of her spine, his fingers stroking her beneath her coat. She wanted him to touch her breast, ached for it. She was halfway to asking him in when he finally lifted his head and sighed.

"You know how to make it difficult for a man," he murmured.

"Sorry."

He smiled. "Don't apologize. I'll pick you up tomorrow at eight-thirty. Okay?"

She nodded, grabbed her purse, and opened the car door. Giving him a final wave, she ran up the path, let herself into the house, and closed the door.

The tires of the car scrunched on the gravel as he pulled away.

After walking into the living room, she sank onto the sofa. Immediately her gaze fell on a photo of Hugh resting on top of the TV.

She turned and flopped onto her back and covered her face with her hands. She didn't know whether to laugh or cry.

Within minutes, she was doing both.

Chapter Eleven

At eight-thirty the next morning, Cameron drew up outside Noelle's house again.

It had taken him a long time to get to sleep the night before. He'd lain awake for hours, thinking about how it had felt to have her in his arms again, and her lips on his.

He'd been convinced that at the last minute she'd say she couldn't go. There was still time for that to happen. But he'd seen her working through it all the night before. And he'd seen the moment that her feelings for him overrode her guilt and her misgivings. That, and the enticing idea of escaping from her regular life and being treated like a queen. His lips curved up as he got out of the car and walked up the path. He had money in his arsenal, and he wasn't afraid to use it to get what he wanted. There were few people who could resist the draw of wealth.

She opened the door, and he was relieved to see her with her coat and shoes on, and a suitcase in her hand, ready to go.

"You're coming, then," he was unable to hold back, and she flashed him a nervous smile.

"Yep, all ready to go."

He took her suitcase from her and put it in the car while she locked up. Then he held open the passenger door for her. She rounded the car and looked up at him, her green eyes wide.

"Morning," he said softly, moving closer to her. Her silver hair shone in the early morning sunlight. She had a few lines around her eyes now, and a few more around her mouth that showed how much she smiled, but she was still as beautiful as the day he'd met her in the swimming pool.

Every time he looked at her, he felt as if he'd opened an oyster shell on the beach and found a pearl.

"Morning," she whispered.

He slid a knuckle beneath her chin and lifted it so he could look into her eyes. Then, without saying anything more, he lowered his lips to hers.

He gave her a long, sweet kiss that she returned with a sigh, then released her with a smile. "Come on," he murmured, not wanting to overwhelm her this early in the day. They had a whole week together, and he was determined to let the relationship grow at her pace.

He drove them the short distance to the airport and handed the keys of the rental car back to the lad behind the counter. They picked up their bags and Noelle headed for the main check-in counter, but Cameron recalled her with a smile. "No need to queue up," he said.

He led her over to the private terminal, where they were welcomed and taken directly out to the plane. It was a small turbo-prop aircraft, able to seat up to twelve people although there would only be the two of them today. Its cabin was decorated with caramel-colored carpets and cream leather seats in twos facing each other with polished wooden tables in between.

They took their seats and buckled themselves in for takeoff. The flight attendant, a smart young Maori woman who introduced herself as Tia, gave them a menu and told them that after lift-off she would serve them breakfast.

Within ten minutes they were in the air.

Noelle was quiet, but Cameron could see she was impressed by the plane and enjoying the notion of flying chartered. She'd previously told him that she never ate much breakfast, but when Tia came to ask them what they would like from the menu, Noelle asked for the Continental option, and before long she was breaking off pieces of a warm, buttered croissant and sipping her latte as if she flew like this all the time.

"Well this beats normal flying," she said, looking out of the window at the Bay of Islands which lay spread out beneath them, the sea shining like a jewel in the sun, the fields a brilliant shade of green.

"Once I'd flown Premium, I never wanted to go back to economy," he told her. "Then I flew Business Class and First Class. Now I've tried charter flights I never want to wait in an airport queue again."

She sipped her coffee, giving him a curious look. "This is terribly rude. But how rich are you?"

He grinned and took a big bite of a warmed breakfast muffin smothered in butter and strawberry jam. "Difficult to say."

"You don't know?"

"Not really. Marcus takes care of all the finances."

"Are you a millionaire?"

He laughed. "Sweetheart, the company is worth billions."

Her eyes nearly fell onto her croissant. "Billions? You're a billionaire?"

"It depends on your definition. There are different meanings of the word billion."

"Really?"

He nodded. "Long and short scales are two naming systems for integer powers of ten using the same words with different meanings. The short scale is based on powers of one thousand, the long on powers of one million. In those countries that use the long scale, a billion is a million million. That's how it used to be in the UK, although nowadays they tend to use the short scale, the same as the US, where a billion is a thousand million. So yes, if we're going by the short scale, I'm a billionaire."

"So you have a thousand million dollars?"

"Pounds." He tried not to laugh. The exchange rate was almost two New Zealand dollars to the pound sterling.

"Oh my God."

He couldn't hold back a chuckle. "I'm teasing you. It's not like I have the money in my pocket. A good part of it is tied up in the business."

"Even so…" She sipped her coffee, obviously processing the information. "Don't you ever worry that women are only after you for your money?"

"All the time." He smiled at her.

"I'm totally going to marry you now," she said. "I've always wanted to be rich."

She carried on talking about investments and the money she'd received in her father's will as she put some honey on a piece of croissant, but Cameron was only half listening. She'd been joking, but he couldn't stop the little leap of his heart at her words. Was it possible they could have a future together?

He mustn't think about it. He had to concentrate on the fact that he was lucky enough to be with her for a week, and not fixate on what was going to happen when it was time for him to leave the country. It was possible they might get on each other's nerves and he'd be glad to see the back of her.

Deep down, he was convinced that wasn't going to happen, but he knew he'd changed over the years. Maybe she wouldn't like the person he'd become.

At the moment, though, she seemed happy enough to be with him, and they started to relax into each other's company, as the plane soared over hills and valleys, forests and lakes, and passed over the white peak that she told him was Mount Taranaki.

They talked about their businesses for a while, Noelle telling him about her plans to expand the Bay of Islands Brides eventually by opening up other shops across the North Island. Cameron told her more about the San Jose shipwreck, and the issues surrounding the Colombian government refusing to sign a share agreement with the group of investors who'd originally claimed they'd found the galleon.

"The Government of Colombia has classified any information about the location of the San Jose as a state secret," he said.

"How on earth did you land the contract to excavate?" she wanted to know.

"We'd done soil and sea depth studies around the coast and had dealt with the Colombian government all the way. We're very careful with whom we share information, and the government were impressed with our record keeping and general security. We'd built up a reputation in Spanish-speaking countries, and I guess we must have been top of their list when they came to look for a company to oversee the task."

She pushed away her empty plate and leaned back in her seat, shaking her head. "You've come such a long way. Who'd have thought you'd be head of a billion-dollar company when you were twenty? I knew you had ambition, but I'm amazed by what you've achieved."

He was human enough to feel flattered by her admiration. "Do you think I've changed much?"

Her green eyes surveyed him, her gaze passing over his face and slipping down his body like the brush of a feather, making him tingle all over. "Physically, a little I suppose. You were always on the slender side, but you've filled out now."

"Are you saying I'm fat?" he teased.

She laughed. "Not at all. You're still very… trim." Her eyes met his, filled with amusement.

"So I have changed in other ways?" he asked.

She thought about it. "I'll have to wait until I get to know you better. On the surface of it… not really. You were always confident. Courageous. Willing to take risks."

"You used to be like that too," he pointed out.

Her smiled slipped a little. "Not so much now."

He cursed himself for his statement. He wasn't going to keep talking about the past. It was pointless; they'd only sadden themselves with the memory of what they'd lost and the reminder of how they'd aged.

Leaning forward on the table, he let his lips curve up as he looked into her eyes. "Enough about me. Let's talk about you."

She looked at the table and fiddled with her coffee cup. "It's probably best if we don't talk about how I've changed."

"On the contrary. Let's start with your hair. Do you dye it?"

"No."

"It's the most beautiful silver I've ever seen. Mine's gone such a dull gray. But yours shines. And that bob suits you." When she was younger, she'd had long brown hair. He'd enjoyed running his fingers through it, and it had always felt like a handful of silk ribbons. Generally gray hair was coarser, but hers still looked as if it would feel silky soft.

"And your figure," he continued. "I can't believe you've had five children. Are you sure they're not all adopted?"

She gave a short laugh. "Thank you for the compliment."

"You don't believe me."

"I think I look okay with my clothes on."

"Take them off and I'll give you my honest opinion."

She chuckled and poked his hand with a fork. "You're such a tease."

"I don't say things I don't mean, you should remember that about me at least." The purse of her lips told him that she did indeed remember how he always said what was on his mind. He'd never been one for false flattery. "You've stayed slim and sexy," he said.

She rested her head on a hand. "I eat healthy food when I can." She shot her empty plate a guilty look. "And I exercise."

"You still swim?"

"Yes, in the summer. I also do Pilates, and I walk a lot. But, like all women I guess, when I look at myself it's difficult to overlook the changes that have happened."

"Maybe they're not as big as you think they are."

"Maybe. I have to say that I think it's tougher for women, though. I'm not saying that men don't struggle with coming to terms with the ageing process. There are enough articles written on the midlife crisis that it's obviously a phenomenon. But it's much more of a physical process for women. Coming to terms with the fact that I'm past childbearing age is hard, even though I don't want any more children."

Of course, he hadn't considered that. "You're going through the menopause?" he asked gently, not sure if she was comfortable discussing it with him.

But she nodded and said, "Yes. I haven't had a period for over a year now. It's been a lot easier on me than on some of my friends. Some women have terrible trouble with mood swings, hot flashes, all sorts of things. I wonder sometimes whether dealing with Hugh's death masked a lot of the emotional symptoms. I've been better the last six months or so. It helps having Emily—my granddaughter—around, as she comes to stay a lot, and I'm often at the school picking her up. And now the girls are going to start having babies. Keeping busy helps. It staves off that feeling of not being needed anymore, of being done, you know?"

He nodded. "I do, although it's different for men, as you said. I suppose it's more of a vanity thing, noticing the changes in our bodies and hair, comparing ourselves to younger guys and finding ourselves wanting. Not being able to do the things we used to do. Accepting that we're not twenty, or thirty, or even forty, is a hurdle we all have to get over at some point. We just have to hope we handle it with some grace."

"At least you haven't lost your hair," she teased.

He ran his hand through it. "It's a lot thinner than it used to be on top! But it's not all falling out."

"No, you don't have a wide parting."

"Ha! I'd shave it all off if that happened. I wouldn't have a comb-over."

They both started laughing, and when he held out his hands she slipped hers into them. "Neither of us is twenty," he reminded her. "But there's some comfort in that. We don't have to impress anyone anymore."

"Not even each other?"

"No. Our souls don't age. Your spirit will always be the same as it was at eighteen—fun, carefree, laughing."

She gave him a wistful look. "I'm not sure it is, but it's nice that you think so."

He squeezed her fingers, then released her hands. "I do. And I think we're coming into Wellington, so we'd better buckle ourselves in."

Chapter Twelve

Noelle's head was in a whirl. She felt like the Queen, or like a famous movie star. It wasn't just the plane, although that was certainly a breathtaking experience. In the past, flying had involved cramming herself into cattle class next to mothers with crying babies or overweight people whose flabby bodies spilled over into her seat. Travelling on a plane with Cameron, waited on hand and foot by the beautiful Tia, was a journey she would never forget.

Next was the gorgeous chauffeur-driven Bentley that collected them from the airport and delivered them to their hotel. She'd never been in such a beautiful car. And she'd certainly never had a chauffeur! And as for the hotel... Knowing that Cameron wanted to impress her, she'd expected that he'd book somewhere flashy, probably one of the larger hotels. She was surprised when they turned up at The Brandon—its sign out the front declaring it was Wellington's only five-star boutique hotel. As they got out of the car and a porter came to collect their bags, she tried to look as if she was used to this lifestyle, hoping her eyes didn't actually pop out of her head onto the floor at any point.

They went inside and up to the desk, and Cameron gave his name, and the receptionist was all smiles as she told him that the Residence Suite was ready for him, and the porter would take their bags up. Noelle remained silent as they followed him into the elevator, but her heart banged on her ribs as they ascended to the eighteenth floor. A glance at the leaflet in the foyer had told her that the Residence Suite was the hotel's premier suite.

She was staying in a premier suite in a five-star hotel! Holy shit!

But he'd promised her a separate room? What did that mean?

Surreptitiously, she cast Cameron a glance while he chatted to the porter about the latest All Blacks rugby game. Her old flame wasn't particularly tall, he was fifty-four, and although she thought him handsome, he wasn't sickeningly good-looking. But there was something about him that had drawn the gaze of the women in the foyer when they'd arrived. It was his confidence, she thought; he'd always had it, and he wore it like a coat. Mingled with the sensual suggestion of wealth, it was an irresistible aftershave. He walked as if he didn't give a fig what other people thought of him. He didn't need anyone else's approval to tell him that he'd done well in life, that he was a success.

And yet, was he happy? He was laughing now, showing his straight white teeth at a comment the porter had made, his natural bonhomie immediately winning the man over. But he'd implied his personal life was empty; his wife had cheated on him, and he wasn't close to his children. In that sense, was he wealthier than she was, or was it the other way around?

The elevator pinged, the doors opened, and the porter gestured for them to exit before him. Cameron walked across to the door of the suite, slid his key card into the lock, and they went inside.

Noelle stopped and stared around, unable to stop her jaw sagging. The small entrance hallway led into a spacious lounge with a huge TV on the wall, two large light-gray sofas with black-and-white cushions, and a glass table with a gorgeous arrangement of fresh flowers. The windows overlooked the city, and the bright sunlight bounced off the water in Lambton Harbour, filling the room with light.

Behind the living room was a dining area housing a long wooden table with six cream chairs and more fresh flowers, and next to that, a full kitchen with every piece of equipment a person could need.

"Do you like it?" Cameron asked, somewhat anxiously.

Not answering, she walked through the living room and discovered that there were two separate bedrooms, each with an *en suite* bathroom. "Which would you prefer?" he asked, following her into the first, which had a stunning view of the Thorndon Hills. "I think you should take this one," he said. "It's a bit bigger, and the other one overlooks the city, so this has a better view."

She turned and looked up at him. Then, still without saying anything, she walked up, slid her arms around his waist, and rested her cheek on his chest.

"Aw," he said, and hugged her back. "Have you gone soft in your old age?"

"It's beautiful," she whispered. "I've never stayed anywhere this nice."

"It's only what you deserve."

She lifted her face to look up at him. "I'm not here because of the money, Cam."

"I know."

"I don't want you to think that at any point."

"Jeez, I remember you well enough. I know what you're like. I'm pleased you're here at all."

She glanced past him—their bags were inside the door, which was closed, so the porter must have retreated discreetly.

She looked up at Cameron. His eyes were nearer to blue than violet in the bright sunshine, reminding her of the sky over the Bay of Islands on a warm summer evening.

"I'm so glad you came to New Zealand," she whispered.

"Me too." He lowered his head until their lips were nearly touching, waited a moment as if wondering whether she was going to pull away, and when she didn't, he moved the last fraction of inch and kissed her.

Noelle closed her eyes and gave herself up to the kiss. The room was quiet and warm, and she could smell the fresh flowers on the chest of drawers, along with the seductive scent of his aftershave. This was a different kiss to the one they'd had in the car the night before. Then he'd claimed her mouth, almost demanding the kiss; this time his lips were featherlight, as if she were a deer in the forest and he was afraid of frightening her away. She appreciated his gentleness, and the fact that he was letting her proceed at her own pace. If he'd picked her up and thrown her on the bed, she'd have run a mile. Probably. He was an exceptionally good kisser, and her body was already responding to him regardless of her mind telling it to slow down.

When he eventually lifted his head, his eyes were full of smiles.

"What's the time?" she asked, somewhat dreamily.

He checked his watch. "Eleven."

"What time is the lunch?"

"One o'clock, but it's here, in the restaurant, so we don't have to go anywhere. I did promise Marcus that we'd meet him and Rebecca in the bar at twelve-thirty though, to catch up first."

"Of course." At least she'd met Marcus already; if his wife was half as nice, everything would be fine.

"How about a coffee?" he asked. "On the balcony?"

"That would be lovely."

He took her hand and led her through to the kitchen and proceeded to make them both a coffee from the machine in the corner.

"This is an amazing kitchen," she said, leaning on the worktop. "I wonder how many people actually use it? If you can afford to stay here, wouldn't you always take advantage of the restaurant?"

"I doubt many people cook for themselves," he replied, watching the hot coffee flow into the mug. "Most will ask a chef to come up from the restaurant to prepare for them." He finished making the coffee and brought it over to her, then laughed at the look on her face. "What?"

"You'd seriously ask a chef to come up here and cook for the two of us?"

"Of course. Why not?"

"Oh my God. That would be so weird."

"Why? I've always found that chefs enjoy taking the time to prepare a single meal. It's a different challenge from running a whole restaurant."

She waited for him to make his coffee, and they took them through the sliding doors in the living room and outside onto the large balcony that overlooked the city. She sat at the elegant table and chairs, the breeze carrying the smell of the sea, intermingling with the aroma of her coffee, a most pleasant mixture.

She sipped from the cup, casting him the odd glance, and in the end his lips curved up in a wry smile.

"What?"

She put down her mug. "I have to ask. Do you do this a lot, then? Have chefs cook for you and… female friends, in your room?"

His expression softened. "Not at all. Usually I entertain business associates; it's more private than eating in the restaurant, and you can have your laptops open or do a presentation at the same time if you want. Sometimes if Marcus has Rebecca with him, we'll eat together. If it's me and Marcus, we'll probably go out somewhere. We have a weakness for Indian food."

She couldn't be sure he wasn't lying, but she thought he was probably telling the truth, and she was pleased. The thought of him doing this with other women made her uncomfortable.

"So if you do invite women up to your room, it's usually for the night?" she asked.

He scratched his cheek. "Mostly for an evening. They don't usually stay."

"For sex," she clarified, thinking how sad it was that his partners didn't stay the night to cuddle up and hold him.

Another wry look. "Well we don't play Scrabble."

"I meant do you talk much?"

"I like to think I'm polite enough to hold a conversation before I ask a lady to take her clothes off."

"Cam…"

He studied her for a long moment, his amusement fading as he obviously realized she wasn't teasing. "I'm not sure I can explain how busy I am," he said eventually. "Although I still work on excavations myself, I'd say eighty percent of my job is overseeing projects, which involves flying from city to city around the world. I rarely stay in the same place more than a week, and often it's only a night or two. Until recently, I've been married, so even though I might have had company, I've had no intention or interest in developing a relationship."

He leaned forward on the table, apparently earnest that she understand. "It's not like it happens every night. Or every week. Or even every month. The last time I slept with someone was a good… I don't know… five months ago? Maybe even six. Occasionally what's happened is that I've met someone, usually through business, and it's become obvious that the attraction is mutual, and we've let nature take its course, and then we've said goodbye. Sometimes we've kept in contact, but usually one of us has been off somewhere new the next day, and that's that. It fulfils a physical need, that's all, and anyone who says it's only guys who don't connect sex with emotion is very wrong. I know it must seem strange to you, having been with only one man the last thirty years, but all I can say is that it's always mutual, I don't pay for it, and it's not a big part of my life. It's… essential. Does that make sense?"

"I suppose so." She turned her coffee mug in her hands. "It's very alien to me. After Hugh died, I came to the conclusion that I would probably never have sex again, unless I was lucky enough to meet and fall in love with another man, which seemed unlikely at the time. The idea of going with someone to satisfy a physical need is alien. I can do that by myself."

Cameron's eyebrows rose, and she realized he was thinking about what that meant, and possibly picturing her doing it.

"Jesus," she said. "You haven't changed a bit. You still have a one-track mind."

"I'm a man. Of course I have a one-track mind."

"I thought men changed when they grew old."

"I'm not old. I'm like fine wine. Or mature cheese."

"Covered in mold?"

They both chuckled.

Noelle smiled at him. The truth was that she had thought that men's sex drives declined later in life. And maybe that was true for Cameron—once in six months wasn't a lot, after all—but clearly sex was still important to him. And of course just because he'd only had sex once in that time didn't mean he didn't do a little DIY on a more frequent basis.

It was her turn to glaze over at the thought of him taking himself in hand. He'd done that for her on more than one occasion, and she'd found it an incredible turn on.

She blinked rapidly and tried to focus.

"Are you worried that you are one of many on a long list?" he asked softly.

"Maybe. I don't know how I feel about that."

He picked up her hand and kissed her fingers. "Over the years, I've developed a certain patter, I admit, in business, to smooth things over and get people talking. But I've never been great at chatting up women. I'm too impatient, and I hate insincerity. If there's been a connection, it's happened naturally. I don't lie to get women in my bed. So you can believe me when I say that this…" and he gestured around the room, "isn't normal. I've never invited a woman to come to a business meeting as my partner. I've never invited one to stay with me for a week. And I've never…" He hesitated for a moment. "…felt this excited to be with anyone. Ever."

His gaze held hers. He was including his wife in that list.

Noelle didn't know what to say. She was immensely flattered. But it was also a huge amount of pressure. She felt overwhelmed, giddy, and flustered all at the same time.

He leaned back in his chair. "Anyway, enough from me. I'm talking too much and boring myself. Tell me, who's running the bridal shop while you're away?"

"My friend, Cathy," she replied. "She covers for me when I go to Auckland on business."

They chatted for a while about their work, Cameron asking questions about the running of the shop, her plans for expansion, and the marketing plan that her daughters' friend Libby was currently working on. Noelle answered his questions, always happy to talk about her job, and somewhat relieved that he'd changed the subject. Being the focus of his attention was daunting, like being an ant under a magnifying glass in the hot sun. She could feel her skin begin to crisp when he stared at her with those intense eyes.

They talked until twelve, and then she said she'd like to get ready for lunch, so they took the cups into the kitchen and then she wheeled her suitcase into her room and shut the door, relieved to have her own space. She'd lived on her own for a long time now. It would be strange to share with someone again.

She looked around the room, opening the large built-in wardrobe and the drawers, then went into the bathroom. It was all shining taps and marble, with a large variety of complementary products lined up. There was also a huge bath. Big enough for two.

She went back into the bedroom, sat on the bed, flopped back, and covered her face with her hands. What on earth was she doing? This wasn't her at all! She was a nice, respectable, middle-aged woman with children and grandchildren. She shouldn't be jet-setting—literally— around the country and sharing a room with a man she'd only just met!

Her heart raced and her chest heaved, but she forced herself to take deep breaths until her pulse slowed down. She hadn't only just met him. And this wasn't some sleazy affair in a dirty motel. She'd gone away with a friend, an old friend who wanted to spend time with her.

The notion of stripping off her clothes, climbing into that huge bath with a naked Cameron, and letting him do all manner of wicked things to her, wasn't even on the cards.

She wasn't going to think about it at all.

Chapter Thirteen

Marcus and Rebecca were already in the bar when Cameron walked in with Noelle at twelve-thirty. He introduced her to Rebecca, who—bless her—welcomed her warmly and said how wonderful it was to meet her at last when she'd heard so much about her. In her early thirties, with a curvy figure and straight blonde hair, Rebecca was one of Cameron's favorite people in the whole world, gentle, kind, funny, and down to earth, perfect for Marcus, who often had his head in the clouds. It was rare for her to leave her kids behind, and he was pleased she and Marcus were able to spend some time alone together. He hoped Noelle liked her.

Noelle gave her a bashful smile. Since his speech to her in the room she'd been quiet, and he wondered whether he'd overdone it. Maybe she was treating this week as a fun, extended holiday, and his declaration that he was excited to be with her had been too much.

Well, he couldn't undo it now, so he put it to the back of his mind and ordered a round of drinks at the bar.

"Are you all set for the meeting?" Noelle asked him and Marcus as they sipped their drinks.

"We're ready," Marcus said. "We've already sent the proposal and exchanged a thousand emails. It's more of a formality than anything. We're the only investors here so it's not like we're competing against anyone. It's a final sign-off, a face-to-face meeting to make sure we're serious and professional about it all."

"I wish you'd told me that earlier," Cameron said. "Now I'm worried."

Noelle laughed, and he smiled at her. She'd changed into a navy skirt and jacket with a white blouse, and she looked every inch a professional businesswoman, the perfect companion for such an important meeting. He was proud to have her with him, and he felt oddly comforted to know she was at his side providing support. Lara had rarely gone with him on business, and he'd gotten used to doing everything on his own, so it was great to have some company for once.

For about fifteen minutes or so they went over the details of the proposed contract, and then a member of the reception team came over to tell them that their guests had arrived.

"Shall we?" Marcus said, and they rose and went out into the foyer.

There were two people from Te Papa Museum and four from the Maritime Archaeological Association, and everyone introduced themselves before making their way into the restaurant.

The meal took two hours, and it went better than Cameron could have hoped. Rebecca and Noelle sat opposite him and Marcus, and they chatted to the people beside them, so nobody was sitting there with nothing to say, and the conversation was lively. While he spoke to the woman from Te Papa sitting next to him, he could hear Noelle talking to one of the men from the MAA about underwater archaeology and he could see that the guy was flattered by her attention, running his fingers down his tie and smoothing back what little hair he had left. Amused, he tore his attention away from her and did his best to concentrate on the business, and the time flew by.

By the time they had their coffees, Cameron knew the deal was done. He exchanged a look with Marcus, whose smirk announced he thought the same. Sure enough, when their guests stood to leave, there was a brief, hurried conversation before the head of the MAA announced they would be thrilled to work with Subaqueous on the Hokianga project, and they'd be in touch to discuss more details within the week.

Everyone shook hands and proclaimed their pleasure at doing business, and then the guests said goodbye and left.

The four of them cheered and exchanged hugs and kisses.

"I knew you'd got it as soon as you cracked that joke about the shark crossing the Great Barrier Reef to get to the other tide," Cameron said to Marcus.

"Wins 'em every time," Marcus replied. His face was lit with triumph, and Cameron felt a strange pang of pride and fondness for his business partner. When they'd first met, Subaqueous was a mid-sized operation struggling to find its footing in the world of archaeology, but Marcus had spotted its potential and had worked his socks off to make it what it was now. He put a lot of time and effort into his work, and as Cameron watched him slide his arms around his wife and kiss her, he resolved to ensure the two of them had plenty of time together. He'd hate to see them go the same way as he and Lara because the business had gotten in the way.

"Well done," Noelle said beside him, and he turned to see her smiling up at him with sparkling eyes. "You were amazing. You're such a charmer. They were all lost as soon as they walked in."

"He was doing voodoo under the table," Marcus said.

Cameron chuckled and bent his head to kiss her. "Thank you for being here," he murmured, touching his lips to her.

"You're welcome," she whispered back, a touch of color appearing in her cheeks as Rebecca and Marcus smiled.

"What are you guys up to now?" Rebecca asked. "Marcus and I thought we'd have a walk through Wellington as we haven't been here before, then take a glance around Te Papa Museum."

Cameron raised his eyebrows at Noelle, who nodded. "It's a great museum," she said, "and I think there's a dinosaur exhibition on, if you're into that sort of thing."

He and Marcus admitted a joint fascination with old bones, so they decided to meet back in the foyer in thirty minutes to walk into town. They returned to their suites—Marcus and Rebecca had one on the floor below Cameron's—changed into more casual clothing, and then headed out into the city.

Noelle had changed into a sweater, jeans, and boots, with her thick jacket over the top. Cameron had done the same, choosing jeans and his long black coat, and he was glad of it, as it was a lot cooler than in the Northland. He'd heard the city was nicknamed Windy Wellington, and today there was a sharp bite to the spring breeze, although the sky was free of clouds. They walked through the streets, looking at the shops and talking, then headed toward the waterfront.

She held his hand while they walked. He brushed his thumb across her knuckles, thinking how amazing that, after all this time, they were together, walking through the streets of New Zealand. So many times over the years he'd wondered what she was doing, and who she was with. And now he'd finally found her. How on earth was he going to let her go again?

He couldn't bear to think about it now, so he shoved the thought out of his brain and put his arm around her as they approached the museum, which stood right on the edge of the waterfront, overlooking the harbor. She slid her arm around his waist as if they were eighteen again, and he felt a surge of happiness to have her there.

She turned out to be a useful guide, explaining the layout and taking them through the various exhibits she remembered. He was pleased she'd retained her interest in archaeology they'd shared when they were young, and she admitted she'd read many archaeological books over the years.

"I wanted to keep that connection with you," she told him softly when Marcus and Rebecca wandered off to look inside the Maori meeting house or *marae* with its intricate carving.

He looked down at her, into her bright green eyes. She hadn't walked away from him without a second thought, and forgotten him as soon as she'd left the country. She'd missed him, too, and had obviously thought about him over the years. That, if nothing else, gave him hope.

Sliding a finger under her chin, he lifted it and placed a lingering kiss on her lips. When he raised his head, there was a dreamy look in her eyes, and his pulse sped up a bit.

As they all wandered into the dinosaur exhibition and looked around the reconstruction of the various skeletons, he couldn't stop himself from wondering what was going to happen when they eventually returned to their suite. She'd accepted her separate room happily, and had said nothing to imply she would be interested in sharing his bed that night. He'd told her he didn't expect it, and he didn't... but that didn't stop him from hoping.

Sex might not have been the driving force it had been for him when they were young, but his libido had far from given up the ghost. He'd found her supremely sexy at eighteen, and that hadn't changed at all. When she slipped off her jacket, it was impossible not to notice how her thin sweater clung to her curves, and his mind kept distracting him by suggesting movie-style footage of him lifting the sweater over her head and filling his hands with her breasts.

But, for maybe the first time in his life, he realized that it wasn't just a physical attraction that consumed him. It was the way she responded to his touch and his comments. Her bashful smile, and the pleasure she took from teasing him. It was the feeling that she knew him, as if he always wore a suit of armor, and she was the first woman who knew what he looked like beneath it. Even Lara had rarely peeked beneath the visor, always too busy, it seemed, to get to know the real Cameron.

Although maybe it was he who had been too busy, he thought sadly, remembering her accusations of how inattentive he'd been, and how he'd ignored her.

Conscious that the others had moved onto the next exhibit, he glanced around and saw Noelle across the room, waiting for him. She'd been watching him, and he could see by her steady gaze that she had seen the sadness pass over him like a cloud.

She might have missed him, but she'd gotten on with her life and found happiness. He hadn't. Not really. He'd married, and he'd taken other lovers, but Noelle had always occupied his heart, he thought. That was why Lara hadn't been able to find a space there.

Noelle approached him and held out a hand. "Come on," she said softly. "There's a Tyrannosaurus rex through here you have to see."

He smiled and followed her, but the thought remained with him. She'd been in his heart then, and she owned it still. All this week in Wellington was doing was stirring up his old feelings and emotions and reminding him what he'd lost.

When he'd seen her at the ball, he should have walked off in the opposite direction. Damn Marcus and his interfering nature.

They took another thirty minutes going around the museum, then, on the way back through the city, spotted a multi-screen cinema complex and decided to go in and watch the latest superhero movie. They booked seats in the special Gold Lounge, ordered a couple of pizzas and a bottle of wine, and had them delivered to their seats, which were more like La-Z-Boy armchairs.

By the time they finished, it was nearly eight p.m., so they caught a taxi back to the hotel, and went into the bar for a final drink or two.

It had been a great day, but butterflies flitted in Cameron's stomach as the clock hands ticked around, and he thought about going back to the suite with Noelle. For the first time in his life, he didn't know what to do. She chatted away, but he had the feeling the same thought was on her mind, because she didn't look at him.

He didn't want her to think he wasn't interested in taking her to bed, because that would be the complete opposite of his intent. Equally, he didn't want her to feel pressured into doing anything she wasn't ready for.

He couldn't imagine how she must feel, having been devoted to her husband for so long. He supposed he should be flattered she was there with him at all.

He'd told her he wanted to be with her as a friend, and he was going to have to stick to that. But it was only now that he realized how disappointed he would be if she didn't want to take it further. He wanted her. He ached to hold her, to kiss her, to give her pleasure, and to take pleasure from her. He wanted to show her how much he'd missed her, and what she meant to him, even after all these years.

"One more round?" he asked, and got up to go to the bar.

"I'll join you." Marcus rose and walked up with him, and leaned on the bar beside him as he gave his order.

"What?" Cameron said as the bartender went off to make the drinks, conscious of his friend's gaze on him.

"You all right?" Marcus asked.

"Tickety boo," he said flatly.

Marcus's lips curved up. "Are you nervous?"

"Jesus."

"Want some tips?"

"Fuck off, Marcus."

His friend gave a short laugh, and then threw him a slightly pitying look. "Best of luck."

Cameron blew out a breath. "Thanks. I need it."

"You really don't. She's nuts about you. It's written all over her. She likes you, Cam. You don't have anything to worry about."

"What are we, twelve?" he said gruffly. "Do you want to pass her a note in class?"

"I would if it would help."

"It might, actually."

The two of them exchanged wry smiles.

"I'm too old for this," Cameron admitted.

"Bullshit. You'll still be pulling when you're in your eighties. You're that sort of guy."

Cameron accepted the whisky the bartender slid over to him and took a sip.

"That came out wrong," Marcus said. "You won't need to pull again, not now you've found Noelle."

"We live on opposite sides of the world," Cameron reminded him, thanking the bartender and giving his room number.

"At the moment. But that's not set in stone."

"She's got her family, I've got the business," he pointed out. "We're worlds apart. It's too late for the ride off into the sunset. This is a brief fling. Nothing serious."

"You keep telling yourself that," Marcus said as he picked up his and Rebecca's glasses and walked away, "and you might start believing it."

Cameron scowled and returned to the table. He didn't need Marcus telling him how to run his life. The dude was twenty years younger than he was, young enough to be his son.

He was quiet while they finished their drinks, and he knew he'd soured the mood. Sure enough, he saw Rebecca and Marcus exchange a glance, and then she finished off her wine in two large mouthfuls and they announced it was time they went to bed.

Noelle was quiet too, and she nodded when he asked if she was ready to retire, so they all went to the elevator and rode up to the seventeenth floor.

Marcus said what a great day it had been, and Rebecca said how much she'd enjoyed the afternoon. Then when the elevator door pinged, they exchanged a hug and kiss, agreed to meet in the foyer next morning for breakfast, and went out to their suite.

The doors slid shut, and the elevator ascended another floor.

Noelle was looking at her feet, and frustration boiled in Cameron's stomach. Jesus, he was fifty-four, he should be better at this by now, but he didn't know what to say. The door pinged, and they walked out. He opened the door to their suite, and they went inside.

They stood in the center of the living room, in the semi-darkness, the only light from the nearly full moon outside that cast everything in silver. Noelle finally lifted her gaze to his, and she cleared her throat.

"I think... I'll head off to bed, if that's okay," she said.

It was only nine p.m. Was she really tired? He wanted to ask her, but couldn't find the words. Instead, he forced a smile onto his face. "Of course."

"I've had a lovely day," she said softly, "and I'm so pleased you got the contract."

"Me too. Thank you for coming to the dinner with me. It was nice to have company for once."

They were polite as strangers. He wanted to take her in his arms, to kiss her, and declare how much he'd dreamed about this, but the intervening years were like a chasm between them. No matter how much either of them tried to justify it, she'd walked away from him. Hugh's ghost stood in the shadows, watching them—he could feel him, and he knew she could, too.

"I'm sorry," Noelle said.

Cameron shook his head. "Good night. I'll see you tomorrow."

She nodded, swallowed, then walked into her room and quietly closed the door.

He stood there for a moment. Part of him wanted to run over, throw open the door, and declare how he felt. Get it all in the open. But he was worried she would reject him. Again. And he wasn't sure if his heart would cope with that.

Instead, he turned and went over to the kitchen. He'd previously asked them to leave some wine in the fridge in case Noelle fancied a glass, and a bottle of Macallan thirty-year-old single malt rested on the side as he'd requested. It had cost him four thousand dollars, but at that moment he took no pleasure in it.

He poured himself a generous measure, not bothering with water or ice, took it over to the dining area, and turned one of the chairs to face the view of the city. He sat and took a large mouthful of the whisky.

He had a sinking feeling that tomorrow, Noelle would ask to go home. Really, he thought, what was the point in her staying? He might have said it was about being friends, but they both knew that was a lie. When they were a couple, there had been not just fireworks but supernovas that had set them both alight. He wanted to experience that again. He wanted her to love him.

But the timing was all wrong, and it was too late, too late.

He knocked back the rest of the glass, his lips twisting at it seared down inside him. Maybe if he drank enough, it would stop hurting.

It had never worked before. But there was always a first time.

Chapter Fourteen

Noelle sat on the edge of the bed and stared out at the view of the Thorndon Hills, black and slightly sinister in the darkness. Her reflection in the glass looked pale and sad, and it wasn't long before she got up to close the curtains to shut it out.

Coming back to the bed, she turned on the lamp on the bedside table, sat again, and lay back, looking up at the ceiling.

She'd done the right thing. This wasn't going to work. When you were fifty-two, you couldn't fly off with a hot rich guy and expect to feel as if you were eighteen again. She thought she could do it, but she'd changed, and she hadn't taken into account how much. She'd read that a person's cells renew themselves every seven years, so technically the young girl she'd been wasn't buried deep inside her—she'd been replaced one cell at a time, until she was a completely different person. Her body had changed, and not for the better.

She'd once gone with Cathy to a kind of New-Age seminar for 'mature women' called 'Don't Let Age Beat You', where the presenter had talked about the three stages of life—Maiden, Mother, and Crone, and how each one was as important as the other. Afterward, Noelle had remarked to Cathy that she didn't like the notion of turning into a Crone no matter how wonderful this stage of life was supposed to be. Cathy had suggested that Wise Woman was a better term, and since then Noelle had tried to think of herself in that way: the village wise woman, the one whom everyone turned to for advice and help. That was the person she'd become. That was who she was now.

And yet... she didn't feel that way inside. In her mind and spirit, she felt as young as the day she'd walked into the café at the swimming pool and seen Cameron waiting for her. She could remember it so clearly. She'd watched him in the pool, and had been impressed by his physique, his swimming technique, and his good looks, and she'd been thrilled when he'd walked up to her and asked her if he could buy her a Coke. He'd been so young, slim and fit. He wasn't quite the same now, of course, and yet the glint in his eye that had told her he'd like to show her the tricks he knew in the bedroom was still there. He was no different inside either.

What was she afraid of? Well, losing him again—after this week, he would go back to England and she'd stay here in New Zealand. But so what if that was the case? Wasn't it better to have loved and lost than never to have loved at all? At this moment, would it hurt any less if they slept together, and then he disappeared?

She was afraid that she might disappoint him. It was an understandable fear after being with the same man for so long. Everything had headed south over the years, and she'd had five children, for crying out loud; it didn't matter how many pelvic floor exercises she did, nothing was going to be as tight down below as it had been back then. But it wasn't as if Cameron was still twenty. He'd aged too, and he'd made it clear that he wasn't expecting her to have the body of a teenager.

So was it ego holding her back? That was part of it. But she thought of Hugh, and realized that being disloyal was a major factor, too.

He'd gone, though, and sad as it was, he wasn't coming back. She'd get no medals for living the rest of her life alone. No prizes. It wasn't as if he'd died two weeks ago. It had been nearly two years. All her family had encouraged her to come away with Cameron, bar maybe Phoebe, but she had guilt of her own surrounding her father, and anyway, although Noelle loved her children, she knew she mustn't live her life by their rules.

So then. What was left? A general fear of the unknown? She'd never thought of herself as a coward. And she didn't want to live the rest of her life filled with regret at the opportunities she'd missed.

She wanted Cameron, she realized. She wanted to be with him again, and to see if it could be as good as she remembered. She wanted to lie with him, to have him hold her, touch her intimately. To have him inside her. Was it a terrible thing to have sexual desires in your fifties? To dream of sex the way you did when you were in your teens?

The room was quiet, and she couldn't hear him in the living room. Had he gone to bed? She hadn't heard the door, so she suspected he hadn't gone out. She lay there, excitement stirring inside her, and let the realization of what she was about to do bloom inside her like a flower. She was going to have sex with him. Not affectionate, husband-

and-wife, beneath-the-covers and lights-out kind of sex, because he'd never been like that. But passionate, rough, animal, kind of sex.

Hopefully, anyway.

She stifled a hysterical giggle, then bit her lip as nerves fluttered in her belly. Holy shit. Was she really going ahead with this?

Maybe he wouldn't want to know. She must have upset him by walking away. Perhaps he'd had enough, and he'd turn her down if she went back out.

Well, faint heart never won fair man. She had to give it a try.

She rose from the bed, unzipped her case, and studied the contents for a moment. Then she lifted out the item tucked underneath and shook it out. It was a nightdress made of plum-colored satin that came to above her knees, with an inverted V of lace over the breasts, and a negligee of the same color that fell to her calves. It was beautiful and sensual, and sexy, she hoped, without being tarty. She'd bought it only a month before from the Four Seasons, her favorite lingerie shop in Paihia, because she'd wanted to treat herself, but she'd yet to wear it.

She laid it on the bed while she stripped off her clothes and then nipped into the bathroom. She brushed her teeth and sprayed on a little perfume, then came out and put the nightdress on. Finally she added a slick of lip gloss. Then she stood with her hand on the door handle.

Her hand was literally shaking, and she was pretty sure her knees were knocking, too.

Swallowing hard, she opened the door as quietly as she could and walked out, her feet silent on the carpet.

She saw him immediately, sitting at the far end of the dining area, looking out across the city. He'd slunk down in his seat, and propped his feet on another chair. An amber liquid gleamed in a glass on the table, the bottle standing next to it telling her he'd planned to be there a while.

Her heart went out to him. He'd told her *I've never felt this excited to be with anyone*. He'd loved her and lost her, and she'd rejected him all over again.

Her nerves dissipated, and she walked through the living room and into the dining area.

Cameron glanced up as she entered, his expression wary, as if he expected to see her in her coat, about to declare she was going to leave.

And then he saw what she was wearing. His eyebrows rose, and his eyes widened.

Noelle didn't say anything. She walked around the table, looking over at the city lights as she did so, seeing the city glowing in the darkness, the moon hanging overhead, silver against the black velvet sky.

He'd sat up a bit and removed his legs from the chair as if hoping she'd sit there. She didn't. She stood in front of him, reached over and picked up his glass, and took a big mouthful of whisky. Dutch courage, she whispered to herself. It seared down inside her, making her catch her breath. He watched her, his eyes dark, still a little wary; he didn't know what she was going to do or say.

Not saying anything, not smiling, she moved closer to him. She placed the glass back on the table. Then she hitched up the nightdress a little, lifted a leg over him, and straddled him, sitting on his lap.

Cameron inhaled, but he didn't say anything. His hands rested on her hips, but he didn't attempt to touch her anywhere else, maybe even now afraid he'd misunderstood. Instead, he looked up at her, his violet eyes almost black in the semi-darkness.

Noelle cupped his face in her hands and brushed her thumbs over the slight stubble on his cheeks. She studied his face—the face she knew so well, and yet hardly at all, with its new fine lines on his brow and the deep creases at the corner of his eyes, a faded scar on his temple, and his gray hair that made him elegant and distinguished and somehow wonderfully sexy at the same time.

"I'm sorry," she whispered, knowing she'd hurt his feelings by walking away from him, both the first time, and earlier, in the living room.

His expression softened, a touch of a smile curving his lips. She stroked her thumb across them, wondering if his heart was racing as much as hers. Then she bent her head and kissed him.

He sighed, his breath whispering across her lips, and closed his eyes. She pressed her lips gently to his, taking her time, and when she eventually touched her tongue there, he opened his mouth and allowed her in, and their tongues slid together in a sensual dance that sent shivers running down her back.

She gave a soft moan, and it was Cameron's undoing, because his hands slid around her back, pulling her tightly against him, and he tipped his head to the side, slanting his lips across hers.

Ohhh... she'd dreamed about this, his fierce passion, his ardent desire. Maybe that, more than anything, was what she'd missed over the years. Hugh had loved her, had enjoyed making love to her, and had never looked at anyone else, as far as she knew, but he'd never craved her like this, never kissed her as if he was afraid to let her go in case she vanished from his arms. Never made her feel as if there was nothing in the world he'd rather be doing than holding her, loving her.

She sank her hands into Cameron's hair, losing herself in the kiss, in the intimacy of the connection that she hadn't had for so long. There was nothing like kissing a man, feeling his bristles against her skin, the smell of warm male blended with his spicy aftershave, the taste of whisky on his tongue. It was the differences between men and women that she loved—the strength in his arms, the muscles in his shoulders and chest, and the feel of him hard against her stomach through his jeans.

"I need you," she whispered against his lips, and kissed up his jaw, along his cheekbones, over his eyebrows, around to his ear. "I want you."

His breaths came fast—he was as turned on as she was, to her relief. "I want you too," he murmured, the first thing he'd said since she'd come out, his voice husky with desire. "So much."

"I'm sorry." She couldn't help but say it again as she returned her lips to his mouth. "I'm... nervous, I suppose. I've never done anything like this. But I want to. I've missed you, Cam. I know you probably don't want to hear it, but I have regretted leaving you, many, many times." Tears pricked her eyes. "If I had to make the decision again, maybe—" She stopped, because he'd put two fingers on her lips.

He shook his head. Then he kissed her again.

She wrapped her arms around his neck and held him tightly, trying to tell him with the kiss how she felt, how much she'd missed him, how much she wanted him. She'd held it in, all these years, she thought, the feelings she'd had for him, all the love, locked away in a corner of her heart that Hugh had known was there, and had never tried to claim. And now the padlock had vanished, and the box was open, and all the feelings were floating out, winding around her like smoke, bringing back memories of how it had felt to be with Cameron, and how much she'd loved him.

Still kissing her, he stroked his hands up her back, around her ribs, hesitated, and then cupped her breasts, which were outlined by the lace bodice, and ached for his touch. He held them for a moment, his thumbs stroking the lace, and then he brushed across her nipples, making her arch her back and moan against his lips.

He groaned in response, and the heat between them rose several degrees as she crushed her lips to his, her body throbbing with need.

"Slowly," he scolded, trying to hold her hips and stop her rocking against him. "You're not making it easy for me."

"I don't want to make it easy." She held his face and looked fiercely into his eyes. "I don't want nice sex, Cam. I don't want husband-and-wife, tender, affectionate sex. It doesn't have to be like that. Does it?"

Chapter Fifteen

Cameron had been prepared to take it slow. To be tender and gentle, because it had been so long since they'd been together, and they needed time to reconnect and rediscover each other.

But Noelle's eyes were filled with desperation, and maybe a touch of fear. And he thought he understood why. She didn't want the kind of sex she'd had with her husband. Maybe because she didn't want to be reminded of him. But also, and she hadn't admitted it in quite so many words, but he had the feeling that Hugh hadn't been experimental in the bedroom. They'd had five kids, so obviously something had worked between them, but making a baby was relatively simple in terms of technique, and it was possible that that had been the extent of Hugh's skills.

In the year Cameron had spent with her, they'd tried pretty much everything that two consenting adults could do on their own, and there had been nothing she'd shied away from, and nothing she hadn't enjoyed. That was what she wanted.

And then it struck him. She wasn't thinking about this as anything more than a fling. *I've never done anything like this*, she'd said, and she'd meant she'd never had a one-night stand, never had an affair. She had no intention of even considering it could be something more.

And why should she? How on earth could it work?

In his heart, he'd hoped for more. He'd been prepared for tender, heartfelt sex, for it to be the first of many times, the beginning of something sweet and beautiful. The start of a future together.

But it was a mirage in the desert, a bittersweet fantasy with no substance. He had to take what she was offering, or nothing at all.

And nothing at all wasn't an option he was interested in.

A hot, sexy fling it was, then. Until he could work out how to make it more than that.

Holding her tightly, he pushed to his feet, making her gasp, and slowly let her slide down him until her feet touched the floor. Then, a step at a time, he began to move her backward to the bedroom.

"No," he told her silkily as he watched her eyes widen. "It doesn't have to be like that."

"We can do it here if you like," she said, putting her hands on her chest to stop him moving, her voice breathless.

He moved forward again, forcing her to step back. "I'm not going to fuck you on the table, Noelle. Not this time, anyway. I understand what you're asking, but I want you in my bed, and I'm going to have you in my bed, so do as you're told."

It was a gamble; they'd indulged in power play all the time back in the day, him taking charge in the bedroom, her pretending she was appalled by his bossiness but secretly loving it, and he'd rolled the dice, hoping she'd join in the game. He could see in the glitter of her eyes and the curve of her lips that she understood, the rapid rise and fall of her breasts telling him it still turned her on.

"No," she said, and he laughed and caught her hands in his, linking their fingers as he continued to back her up. She met the wall next to his bedroom door with a bump and a gasp. He lifted their hands, pinning hers above her head, and kissed her, not bothering to hold back this time, letting the full heat of his desire consume them both.

Noelle moaned and opened her mouth to let him plunge his tongue inside, and he pressed up against her, driven half-crazy by the softness of her body in the satin nightdress. Releasing her hands, he dropped his to her thighs and slid his fingers up beneath the nightdress and onto her bare bottom, his already stiff erection hardening to rock at the feel of her naked skin, as silky as the satin.

Her hands were in his hair, fingers clenching, her body straining against him. Unsure whether it was the couple of whiskies he'd had, or the mixture of need and want and hormones and pheromones, he lost the plot a little, all thoughts of being gentle and tender fleeing his mind. All he could think about was how much he wanted her, and how he needed to be inside her, driving them both to a fast and furious release.

Pulling her away from the wall, still kissing her, he moved her back through the bedroom door, flipping on the switch which turned on the lights above the bed. She was already pushing up his sweater, and he helped her tug it over his head and let it drop to the floor. She started unbuttoning his shirt, and he kissed her while she pushed the buttons through the holes, pleased at the urgent fumbling of her fingers, and the way her breasts rose and fell with her rapid breaths.

Reaching the bottom, she pushed the sides of his shirt apart, and ran her hands over his chest. "Mmm…" she murmured, her fingers skimming over his nipples, exploring his muscles. "You're in fine form, Cam."

He didn't work out in front of a mirror or anything, but he had to keep fit as part of his job, and he swam most days, so it was nice that the effort was appreciated. He undid his belt and slid down the zipper of his jeans, and she pushed them over his hips and let him take them off with his socks.

Clad in only his tight black boxer-briefs, he undid the tie at Noelle's waist, slid the pretty negligee off her shoulders, and tossed it onto the chair. The satin nightdress skimmed over her breasts and hips, and his fingers itched to slide beneath it, onto her smooth skin.

He held the hem, but for the first time he felt her tense in his arms. She didn't say anything, but he could sense her reluctance to take that last, final step, to bare herself to his gaze. She wanted to play this as if it were a wild, wicked affair, but it was her first time with someone other than her husband for thirty years, and she was woman enough to be nervous about it.

His heart went out to her. Letting the nightgown go, he moved her back a few steps, then turned her to face the window overlooking the city, moving up close behind her. He hadn't yet pulled the curtains, and he steered her up against the window, lifting her hands so she rested both palms on the glass.

The smell of her perfume wound around him, as intoxicating as the whisky. He was inches from throwing her onto the bed and plunging into her. He wanted her so badly it was taking all his self-control to slow himself down. No matter what she said, he wasn't going to let it last seconds. Having her there was like Christmas Eve—the anticipation was part of the attraction, and he wished he could hold onto this moment forever, knowing he was about to have her in his arms, to be inside her.

He stroked down her, his hands gliding easily over the satin nightgown, then returned his hands up to her breasts. They were soft and heavy in his palms. He brushed his thumbs over her nipples, and her lips parted in a silent sigh.

"I want you," he said huskily, kissing her shoulder, her neck, up to her ear. "I've thought about this every day since you left. I've hungered for you. Dreamed about you in the darkness." It was true. Noelle might have been able to put him out of her mind when she bedded her husband, but he'd been unable to do that. She'd haunted him for thirty years, and he was ready to lay that ghost to rest.

A moan escaped her lips as he teased her nipples with his thumbs and forefingers, her head tipping back onto his shoulder. "Cam…"

"I used to love making you come," he said, his tongue lacing over her skin, sending shivers down her back. "Over and over. Do you remember?"

"Yes…"

"I want to do it again. I want to hear you sigh my name. Will you do that for me?"

"Mmm, yes…"

"While I'm inside you," he said, dropping his hands. "The first time. After that, I'll play with you all night, if you want."

She blinked, focusing on their reflections in the window, and he watched color stain her cheeks. "Um… I should get—"

"I've got condoms," he told her, kissing her ear.

"No, I mean, I brought some… um… lubrication…" she began. She then gave a half laugh, half gasp as she saw his eyebrows rise in the reflection. "No! Cameron! Jeez. You haven't changed! You're still…"

He nuzzled her ear. "Gorgeous? Handsome?"

"Wicked," she corrected with a sigh. "Naughty."

He shrugged and sucked the lobe. "You say potato…" He nipped her earlobe and made her gasp. "Why would you need lube?"

Her lashes lowered. "It's just… at my age, sometimes I need a bit of help."

"We won't need it," Cameron stated.

She glanced over her shoulder with a short laugh. "That's quite an arrogant thing to say."

He tugged on her nipples, and she closed her eyes and moaned. "Prove me wrong, then," he murmured. He ran his fingers up the outside of her thighs, over her hips beneath the nightgown, across her soft belly, and then over her mound. She held her breath as he paused, and then he slid his fingers down, into the heart of her.

"See?" He spoke smugly as he found her wet and swollen, more than ready for him, but he was almost shaking with need.

She closed her eyes and gave a little shake of her head.

"You were always easy to arouse," he said hoarsely, kissing her ear, "if a man knew which buttons to press." He swirled his finger over her clit, and she moaned.

His body superheating, Cameron turned her, pushing her up against the glass. He bent and kissed down over the lace V of the gown to her breasts, and took each nipple in his mouth in turn, sucking the tender skin until the material was soaked through and she squirmed against him. At the same time, she skimmed her hands over his shoulders and down his back, and then over his hips, her fingers closing around his erection through the cotton underwear.

"Always hard," she whispered.

"For you." His breaths came fast as she stroked him, her fingers sure and steady. What he wouldn't give to let her stroke him to a climax, or to drop to her knees and close her mouth around him. There were so many things he wanted to do. He wanted to kiss down her body and bury his mouth in her. Lick and suck her to an orgasm.

But not this time. This first time, he wanted to be inside her, looking into her eyes when they came.

When she didn't stop, he took her wrist and moved her hand away.

"Come in my hand if you want," she teased, nibbling his bottom lip with her teeth, and tugging her wrist and trying to free herself. "Or over me. I don't mind."

"Jesus." He moved back and, while she watched with wide eyes, shed his underwear. Grabbing a condom from the bedside table, he ripped the packet off and rolled it on, then came back to her.

"Spoilsport," she said, reaching for him again.

He turned her so her back was to the bed and, taking her by surprise, he peeled the nightgown up her in such a quick, smooth move that it was off before she could stop him. She gasped, her hands automatically coming up to cover herself, but he pushed her so that she stumbled and fell backward, bouncing on the mattress. She squealed, but he moved on top of her, between her legs, and looked down at her.

"If you think I'm coming anywhere but inside you, you can think again." He grasped her hands in his and pinned them above her head.

Noelle looked up at him, her pupils so large that her eyes looked black. Her lips were parted, her breasts rising and falling quickly.

He raked his gaze down her, the years falling away as he remembered another time like this years ago. They'd been out with friends, and she'd taunted him all evening, whispering things she wanted to do to him in his ear, rubbing her foot up his leg under the table, driving him crazy. As soon as he'd taken her to his room at uni, he'd thrown her on the bed, pinned her down, and thrust them both to a shuddering climax. It was possibly the best sex they'd had, and he could see in her eyes that she remembered it too.

God, he'd missed her so much. And she hadn't changed a bit. She was still as beautiful as she had been back then, and she still made his heart leap when she looked at him like this, with desire in her eyes.

"Tell me to stop," he said roughly. "Tell me you don't want this."

"I do," she whispered fiercely.

He'd hoped she would say those words to him in another context, but it had never come to pass. At that moment, though, he was more than happy with their meaning this time.

Chapter Sixteen

Cameron held her gaze, and Noelle flexed her fingers in his, her heart thudding, loud in her ears. His eyes were like lasers, so hot she felt they might sear through her flesh. He'd always been passionate like this, demanding, but she was touched and awed that he still felt desire for her, still wanted her, after all this time.

He kissed down her neck to her breasts and took a nipple in his mouth, and she closed her eyes and moaned, clenching inside. He'd teased that she was easy to arouse, and it was true, when she was in his arms. He sucked and licked the sensitive skin, and she knew she couldn't take much more.

"Cam…"

He pushed up to look at her and his lips curved up. Bending, he kissed her, more tenderly than she'd expected as he moved his hips and pressed the tip of his erection into her folds. He was still holding her hands, and she could only wait as, slowly, gently, he pushed his hips forward and sank into her.

It had been a long time since she'd welcomed a man inside her, and the sensation of him filling her up made her gasp.

He stopped immediately, a frown flickering on his brow. "Did I hurt you?"

"No. It's… been a while, that's all." She smiled.

His frown lifted. He bent and kissed her again while he pulled out a little, then eased forward, coating himself with her moisture, going further each time until he was buried up to the hilt.

It was a delicious feeling, and when he stopped and closed his eyes, she knew he was reveling in it too. She did the same and wrapped her legs around his waist, tilting up her hips, and enjoyed the moment, the feeling of being with a man, locked together in the most delicious, animal way possible.

When she opened her eyes, he was looking at her. He held her gaze, and a little part of her thought how strange it was that his violet eyes staring into her own could make her heart give that little skip and suck all the breath out of her body.

Keeping his eyes on hers, he began to move.

Oh God, she was going to come, and he hadn't even started yet. It was because it had been so long, and she was so turned on and excited at being with him...

"Cam..." she bit her lip, trying to fight it.

"Keep your eyes on me," he said, obviously feeling her tense around him. "I want you looking at me when you come."

Her face burned, but there was nothing she could do about it, and the climax swept over her, tightening her around him in pulses. It was impossible to keep her eyes open all the time, but she felt his gaze on her, fiercely possessive, and she knew what was on his mind. He wanted to make sure she was thinking about him, and only him.

So she forced her eyes open, and looked deeply into his as her body continued to feel the aftershocks of the orgasm. Only when she'd calmed did he kiss her, his mouth tender, and she sighed against his lips as he started moving again, already feeling the spark of pleasure begin to build deep inside.

"You're going to sex me to death, aren't you?" she whispered.

He gave a short laugh and kissed her. "Happy to try."

"Cam..."

"I'm going to take my pleasure from you, Noelle Acton, and there's nothing you can do about it, so make yourself comfortable." His hips moved rhythmically, driving him deep inside her. His use of her maiden name confirmed her suspicion that he was reminding her of their previous relationship, of how close they'd been.

"Don't I have a say in the matter?" she mock-protested.

"No." He slowed, grinding against her, and her lips parted in a blissful *Aaahhh*.

He was still holding her down, and she felt a thrill inside at his words, *I'm going to take my pleasure from you...* He didn't mean it; he'd never been selfish in bed and he'd certainly never forced himself on her. But she knew that this was what she'd missed. The power play. Sex wasn't just about achieving orgasm. And it wasn't just about showing your partner tenderness and affection. Those things were important, but it was also fun to explore other things—the differences between men and women, and her age didn't matter; he still turned her on. Still drove her insane with hunger and need.

They kissed, sucking, nipping, their tongues sliding against each other, and he trailed his hot mouth down her neck, lacing his tongue over her skin, down to her breasts. He aroused her again, slowly, always moving inside her, and she felt the inevitable spin toward another orgasm, as if she were climbing a spiral staircase, growing gradually closer to the goal at the top.

It had grown warm in the room, and when he released her hands and she placed them on his body, she found his skin hot and slick where it slid against hers. He placed a hand on her thigh and pulled her leg higher around his waist, and she moaned as he drove deep inside her, taking her closer with every thrust.

"Fuck," he said, and she knew he was close to a climax, his body taking over, his muscles tensing beneath her fingertips. "You're so fucking hot, Noelle. How do you still drive me so crazy?"

"Oh God." She sank a hand into his hair and tugged his mouth down to hers. "I'm going to come. Harder."

He groaned and pounded into her, and they came together, and it made her think of the two seas that met at Cape Reinga, the Pacific and the Tasman, the waves crashing into each other, all that power and wildness blending into one. When there was passion like this, nothing mattered, she thought as he cried out her name. It was stupid to deny it, or to try to fight it, because it was natural and feral, like the seas, and battling it was like trying to keep a ship afloat on the raging waves—you were always going to go under, and it was best to let it happen, to let the waves crash over you, and let the ocean take you down into the darkness.

The intense pleasure faded, their muscles relaxed, and, slowly, gradually, she drifted back into herself. She blinked and felt a little embarrassed at the craziness of her thoughts. It was just sex, she told herself as he bent his head and touched his lips to hers. It wasn't some fantasy ending to a romantic movie with swelling strings and champagne corks popping and all that.

And yet, as he looked into her eyes and smiled, warmth spread through her, and she felt a glow of contentment.

"You're still a good fuck," he said.

Her jaw dropped at his cheekiness, and she smacked his butt. "Mind your language."

He laughed, withdrew, and disposed of the condom. "You have changed. You used to swear more than I did."

"That was before I had kids." She felt a pang of disappointment as he got up. Just sex, she thought. Remember?

But he was only retrieving the duvet, and when he came back with it to find her about to swing her legs over the edge of the bed, he tugged her arm so she fell back, looking upside down at him.

"Don't even think of leaving my bed," he scolded, bending to kiss her. "Now I've got you here, there's no way I'm letting you go."

She closed her eyes, enjoying the movement of his lips across hers, and the fact that he didn't want her to go. "All right."

"Come on. You're cold. Let me warm you up." He held the duvet up while she moved back against him, covered them over, and then pulled her into his arms, right against him, her thigh across his, her breasts to his chest.

He kissed her, then rested his lips on the top of her head. "You have no idea how often I've dreamed about this."

Noelle didn't reply. It felt like a dangerous road to walk down. Admitting that she'd dreamed about him in her bed, that she'd missed him, that she wanted him back in her life—what was the point of that? She had to focus on the fact that this was an affair, a fling, a series—possibly—of one-night stands until it was time for them both to return to the real world. She didn't want to talk too much about before, or what happened next. If there was any time when it was important to live for today, this was it.

He stroked down her back, his fingers light on her skin. "Sorry."

That made her feel guilty, and she kissed his shoulder. "I've dreamed about it too."

"I know." He ran his fingers through her hair.

She didn't want him to think that this wasn't amazing, being with him again. Pushing up onto an elbow, she leaned forward and kissed him, taking her time, while she trailed her fingers through the hair on his chest.

"Are you tired?" she asked, lifting her head to look at him.

He raised an eyebrow. "I might need a minute or two."

She laughed. "I see you're still insatiable. I was going to suggest taking a bath together."

His eyes lit up. "Now you're talking."

"Come on, then. They had some nice bubble bath in there that I want to try."

So she ran the bath for them and poured the milky liquid in until the bubbles foamed. Luckily the taps were in the middle, so Cameron didn't have to take the tap end, and they sat with legs entwined, washing each other slowly while they talked about their day.

"I liked Rebecca," she said as he ran a soapy hand down her leg. "I get the feeling she keeps Marcus grounded."

"Very much so." He lifted her foot out of the water, kissed her toes, then massaged the sole gently with his fingers. "He could easily work twenty-four hours a day; he forgets what the time is and gets caught up in what he's doing. I don't want him to make the same mistake I did, and I told Rebecca that it was important we both make sure he leaves the office at six latest, and that he doesn't work weekends unless it's really necessary. I don't want him to miss his kids growing up, and I don't want him to neglect his wife."

She watched him lower her foot into the water and pick up her other one to massage that. "I'm sorry your marriage failed," she said softly. At least she hadn't had to go through that. "But you shouldn't take all the blame yourself. It takes two to tango, Cam. It takes two to make or break a marriage."

"I was hardly home. I can't even remember the kids growing up. She had every right to complain."

"Did she say so at the time? Was she always begging you to stay?"

He lowered her other foot. "No."

"Did she ask you at any time to sit down and talk to her about your marriage? Did she tell you she was unhappy about where it was going, before she had the affair, I mean?"

"No."

"That's what I'm trying to say. There has to be communication in a relationship. And compromise. I've tried to make that point to all my children. It's not good enough to be irritable with your partner because they're not saying what you want to hear. You have to be open from the beginning. Say what is and isn't working. It happened with Elliot, my youngest boy. He broke up with his partner, Karen, a couple of months ago. I suspected it wouldn't last. He drifted into the relationship, and the two of them were like oil and water; they didn't blend at all. But after they broke up, he admitted to me that they didn't talk, not about things that mattered. He's not a great talker anyway, but he still acknowledged that there needed to be that communication for it to work."

"I can't believe you've got five kids," he said. "You look remarkably good on it."

"Well thank you, kind sir."

"Do you ever think what our kids would have been like?"

Her smile faded slowly. "Sometimes. That's where it gets hard for me. I can't wish away my children."

He frowned. "Of course not."

"And I can't wish I hadn't met Hugh either, because then I wouldn't have my kids."

"I know. That wasn't what I was saying."

She ran a hand through the bubbles. "I know. To be honest, I don't like thinking about alternate realities because it makes my head hurt. I get too mixed up. I don't know what to think or feel."

"Then don't." He reached out a hand and pulled her toward him. "Turn around."

There was just enough room for her to do as he bid, and he pulled her back against his chest, between his legs, and wrapped his arms around her.

"Let's make a pact," he said, kissing her ear. "We're not going to talk about what might, or could, or should, have happened. What's done is done. We're here today, together, and that's amazing to me. I don't want to spoil that by making you upset. Let's concentrate on right here, right now, and make the most of this wonderful moment."

"I'd like that," she whispered, lifting her face for his kiss, her body already beginning to stir as his fingers trailed over her breasts beneath the water.

It was going to be a long night.

Chapter Seventeen

They met Marcus and Rebecca in the foyer the next morning, chose a table in the restaurant, then helped themselves to the huge buffet of continental and cooked breakfasts available.

Cameron was busy heaping scrambled egg onto his plate when Marcus appeared beside him, elbowing him out of the way so he could get to the bacon.

Marcus gave him a sly look and grinned. "I think that's the first time I've ever seen you smile before ten a.m."

"Shut up."

Marcus chuckled. "I'm pleased for you. I feel like a proud father. Just take it easy, a man of your age. You don't want to put your back out."

Cameron placed a couple of sausages on his plate and a slice of toast. "At least if I pull a muscle now I've got someone to massage it for me."

"That's true. It's a sad day when a man doesn't have someone to massage his muscle."

That made Cameron laugh. "I've worked up an appetite, anyway. I'm starving."

"Best way to work off some calories, so they say."

Chuckling, they made it back to their seats and dug into their breakfasts. Noelle had a bowl of muesli and yoghurt, and a croissant and jam to follow, so clearly she was feeling hungry too.

He leaned back as a waitress came over to fill their coffee cups, and his eyes met Noelle's. She chewed her muesli, her eyes dancing as she glanced at his full plate. "Peckish, sweetheart?" she asked when the waitress withdrew.

"Most important meal of the day," he said, "especially when you've had a workout."

Marcus snorted, and Rebecca laughed.

"Actually I was referring to the treadmill," he said wryly. They'd woken early, taken an hour to snuggle up, talk, and eventually make love again, and then he'd run for thirty minutes before coming back up to share the shower with her.

"Yeah, yeah." Marcus munched his bacon and pointed his fork at his wife. "After this, I'm taking you back to the room and making mad passionate love to you. Can't let the old guy beat me."

"I hope you'll let my breakfast go down first," Rebecca said, making them all laugh.

Cameron chuckled. "So what's the plan today?"

Marcus had a sip of coffee. "We'd love to go on the tour of the Weta Workshop, where they did all the models for *The Lord of the Rings*. I've rung up and there are still tickets available, if you'd like to go."

Cameron glanced at Noelle. "What do you think? Marcus and I are big fans of *The Lord of the Rings*. It was the second thing I thought of when I heard we had a project in New Zealand." He smiled.

Noelle blushed. "I'd love to!"

"Cool," Marcus said, pleased, "I'll book those, then."

"How long are you staying in Wellington?" Noelle asked.

"Just tonight," Rebecca replied. "After that we thought we'd go over to the South Island on the ferry, hire a car, and spend a few days driving down the coast. I'd like to visit Kaikoura and do some whale watching, and then go to Christchurch."

"It's a beautiful drive," Noelle told them. "The scenery of the Canterbury plains is magnificent with the Southern Alps behind it, very *The Lord of the Rings*, if you're into that."

"Oh we are," Rebecca said. "We've watched all three extended movies, like, a dozen times, as well as all the extras. I'm really looking forward to it. So what about you two? You're heading north tomorrow, right?"

Cameron nodded and had a mouthful of the hot, strong coffee. "I thought we'd take our time and see a few places as we go."

"If you love Tolkien," Noelle said, "we could go to the Hobbiton set at Matamata."

"Oh yeah," he said enthusiastically. "I'd love that."

She smiled at his fervent reply. "First, though, we should go to Rotorua."

"Is that where there are the mud pools and geysers?" Rebecca asked.

Noelle nodded. "The earth's crust is very thin—some say it's the thinnest in the world—and you can feel the rumbling of the volcanic activity underfoot. There's also a Maori village there you can look around."

"That's settled then," Cameron said with satisfaction.

"When did you two last have a holiday?" Noelle asked with amusement.

He looked at Marcus, who stared back blankly. "Was it 2006?" Marcus asked. "Or 2007?"

Rebecca laughed. "They work hard, the two of them, so it'll be good to have a break. Not that Marcus will ever truly be on holiday." She rolled her eyes as his phone dinged to announce the arrival of an email.

"I'm important," Marcus told her, flicking his thumb over the screen. "It's only you who doesn't seem to realize that."

Rebecca snorted and turned to Noelle to ask her about the best places to visit on the South Island. Cameron smiled and listened to them talk, feeling a deep sense of contentment he hadn't felt in a long time. Contentment through work was one thing, and he felt that almost on a daily basis because he loved his job, but sharing time with friends like this, that happened too infrequently. He was determined to make the most of every moment they had together.

They finished breakfast and headed back to their rooms to collect what they needed for the day. Once they were inside the room, Cameron pulled Noelle into his arms and gave her a long, lingering kiss.

"Don't even think about it," she scolded as he slid his hands down to cup her bottom and pull her tightly to him.

"I can't stop thinking about it." He nuzzled her neck, playing through the memory of how she'd felt in the bath the night before, silky and slippery in his hands. He'd taken his time to arouse her to another climax, enjoying listening to her moans and sighs fill the steamy room. And that morning had been just as wonderful, having her naked in his arms in bed, spending ages kissing and stroking one another before he'd finally given in, pulled her on top of him, and slid inside her. She'd ridden him slowly, her self-confidence growing as she'd seen the admiration in his eyes, and he'd felt almost tearful as he'd come, giving thanks to God, if He happened to be listening, for bringing them together again.

"I'm sure I should be slowing down sexually at fifty-four," he murmured, wishing he had time to take her to bed. "I should be happier with a cup of tea and a good book. But I'm not." His body burned for her. "I'm obsessed. I can't think about anything but you at the moment."

She shuddered, her breath hot on his throat, and he felt the touch of her tongue there, in the hollow, a gesture that for some reason made him hard immediately. "Me neither," she whispered. "I know what you mean. I didn't think it was possible to be insatiable when you were past fifty, but I am." She lifted onto her tiptoes and pressed her nose to his. Her breath brushed across his lips. "A hongi," she whispered. "We've exchanged the breath of life. You're now a *tangata whenua*, one of the people of the land."

He tightened his fingers on her hips as a swell of fierce emotion took him. He couldn't breathe, couldn't swallow, couldn't do anything but stare into her green eyes as the wave washed over him.

He loved her. He still loved her, after all this time. He'd thought that being with her would mean starting all over again, building up that emotion like pouring water into the vessel they'd emptied when she'd gone, but it wasn't. All they'd done was pick up where they'd left off. The vessel was already three-quarters full, and every minute he spent with her he was filling it up, and holy shit that was a mistake because soon it was going to be full, and then what was he going to do?

But he couldn't say anything because he'd promised her they'd make the most of the time they had. Instead, he held her face in his hands and kissed her until she sighed.

"Tonight I'm going to make love to you," he told her, his voice husky, "and I'm going to pleasure you until you beg me to stop."

"Jesus." Her face was flushed, her eyes feverish. "I'm not going to be able to concentrate all day now!"

"That's what I want," he said, somewhat fiercely. "I don't want you to be able to think about anything but me."

Their eyes met. Whatever she saw in his made her inhale and blink, and her lips parted.

"Cameron..." she whispered.

Thinking that she was about to remind him of his promise, he looked away and picked up his jacket. "We shouldn't keep them waiting."

She didn't say anything, just collected her coat and purse, and they made their way down to the foyer to meet Marcus and Rebecca.

For a while he worried he'd come on too strong and he'd upset her, but she laughed at Marcus's jokes and chatted away to Rebecca, and when she looked back at Cameron her eyes were warm, so he thought she'd probably forgiven him.

In the end, they had a wonderful day. They travelled to the Weta Workshop, had a tour of the cave with its props, weapons, and costumes, listened to the documentary, and spent ages in the shop looking at the merchandise. Cameron treated himself to a model of Gandalf for his desk in his London office, much to Noelle's amusement. He also bought his son a couple of items, as they'd watched the movies together once when Josh was in his teens, and got the two girls a pair of paua shell earrings each.

He'd been concerned that Noelle might find the day dull, as not everyone was as nerdy as he and Marcus, but it was obvious from the start that she'd watched the movies many times, and she was as fascinated as he was to look at all the props.

When they'd finished, they stopped at a restaurant for a long lunch, spending a couple of hours talking and getting to know each other. Cameron was pleased that Noelle seemed to get on so well with both Marcus and his wife, and he could tell that Marcus liked her from the way he teased her, which he only did with his closest friends. Marcus had always been polite to Lara and had never criticized her in Cameron's presence, but they'd never been friends, so it was nice to see him take to Noelle so quickly.

While they were eating, Rebecca said that the Royal New Zealand Ballet were doing a special performance of The Nutcracker. "You've all done your nerdy stuff," she teased. "I'd love to see the ballet."

Noelle immediately said she'd love to go, and as Marcus was happy to please his wife, Cameron rang and booked the best four tickets they had left in the front of the dress circle.

They had a look around the shops for a few hours, returned to their hotel room to change, and set off for the Opera House as the sun began to set.

Noelle was quiet, and Cameron wondered if she was remembering a previous trip to the ballet many years ago. They'd gone to see Swan Lake at the London Coliseum, and it had been a magical summer night.

They'd only been dating a few weeks, but on that night Cameron had told her he loved her for the first time.

The thought made him sad. At the time, they'd had no idea of the trials and tribulations coming their way. They hadn't known how much their love would be tested, and that ultimately it wouldn't be strong enough to withstand the pull of her family.

He thought about it all the way through the ballet, wishing he could put it out of his mind, but it was impossible to rid himself of the underlying bitterness. Not toward Noelle, and not even toward her parents, who had forced her to make that decision. Just toward life, or Fate, or God. And maybe toward himself for not making more of an effort to keep her. If he'd been more insistent, if he'd told her he loved her more... Would she have stayed?

The ballet was magnificent, but it reminded him that Christmas was coming, a time of year he didn't look forward to and didn't enjoy. He'd probably end up working through it, he thought as the ballet drew to a close. That was what he usually did. His girls spent the day with their mother, and Josh had a girlfriend now, so no doubt he'd be with her. Rebecca would almost certainly insist he came to their house for the day, and he would consider it, because he loved Marcus's two young kids, and they always made him feel welcome. But this year, he suspected he wasn't going to be good company.

They left the Opera House and took the car back to the hotel, and Marcus and Rebecca gave them both a hug and kiss and said they'd meet for breakfast in the morning before they all headed off. They rode up in the elevator together, and after the other two had exited at their floor, Cameron and Noelle continued to their suite.

He swiped the keycard and let them inside, and Noelle dropped her coat and purse onto the sofa. He thought she might declare she was going to have a bath, or maybe say she was tired and wanted to go to bed. But she didn't. She waited for him to come in, then took his hand and led him over to the window. She stood before him, lifted her arms around his neck, and raised on tiptoes to kiss him.

Then she whispered, "What's the matter, Cameron? Tell me. You've been sad all evening, and I want to make it right."

Chapter Eighteen

Noelle waited for Cameron to answer. He hadn't been grumpy or irritable, just quiet and a touch melancholic, and she wasn't sure what had prompted the mood.

Had he remembered the night they'd gone to the Coliseum? Guys didn't usually retain information like that, in her experience. Hugh had bought her flowers on their anniversary, and jewelry for her birthday, but that was as far as his romantic nature had extended, and they'd never been the sort of couple to whisper sweet nothings long into the night.

It had been Swan Lake, if she remembered correctly. It had been a warm summer night, and even though it was difficult to see the stars in London because of the light pollution, she recalled that the full moon had been super bright, exactly the same as it was tonight, hanging in the sky like a Christmas bauble.

He'd told her he loved her that night. At that moment, she'd thought they'd be together forever. She thought she'd found her Mr. Right. It made her immensely sad that it hadn't worked out.

He hadn't said anything. The silence stretched out between them. His jaw was knotted, his back stiff, and she thought that maybe he was arguing with himself as to whether to admit to her what was on his mind.

Then, all at once, his shoulders released their tension and his expression relaxed, and he moved closer to her, pressing her up against the glass.

"You've cast a spell on me," he said, his husky voice, full of desire, giving her goosebumps. "I don't think I registered a single step of the ballet. All I could think about was you, kissing you, and sliding my hands beneath that dress onto your silky skin." To prove his point, he lifted the hem of her dress, put his hand on the outside of her thigh, then traced his fingers up over her hip.

She sucked her bottom lip and shivered, her heart racing. This kind of thing didn't happen to fifty-two-year-old women! She should be taking off her makeup, putting on her night cream, then climbing into bed and turning off the lights before they even began to kiss. That was what mature people did. Men of his age didn't look at their partners as if they wanted to devour them.

But she knew what he meant. She'd watched the ballet, the elegant men and women acting out the story, but all the time she'd been conscious of the man next to her, the smell of his aftershave, the feel of his breath on her ear when he whispered to her during the performance, the touch of his hand on hers, the brush of his fingers sending ripples of pleasure through her body.

And suddenly she didn't care what people thought of her—what her kids thought, her friends, the people at reception who must have guessed they weren't married. Yes, she'd come away with Cameron for sex. Why should she hide it, or pretend otherwise? He set her alight, and it was foolish to deny it.

She moistened her lips with the tip of her tongue. "What do you want, Cam? You have me here now, tonight. Tell me what you want."

He slid his hands around to her bottom and tightened his fingers there, his mouth brushing over hers. "I want to fuck you."

She gasped, her lips curving up. "Jeez. Say what you mean."

"You asked me. I'm not going to beat around the bush. I want you. I want to fuck you until you come hard. I want to hear you scream my name. Is that so terrible? Does that not fit with your view of middle-age, sweet Noelle?" He chuckled as he kissed her.

He was mocking her, a little; he knew he was shocking her, and that she wasn't used to this kind of sexy talk, or to giving into her urges anymore. She felt a tad resentful, but she wasn't going to show it. Two could play at this game.

"I want you too," she said, beginning to undo his shirt buttons, her fingers trembling a little. "I want to feel you inside me."

He took her bottom lip between his teeth and tugged it gently. "Do you, now?"

She hesitated, looked up into his eyes, and held his gaze. Then she gave a sharp tug, ripping his shirt apart so that buttons flew off across the room.

"Fuck!" He laughed. "That's my girl," he said with satisfaction, and then his lips were on hers, and Noelle felt the world begin to spin off its axis as he plunged his tongue into her mouth.

He kissed her soundly, while she tugged his shirt off his shoulders, and he pulled her dress up her body. They broke apart so he could lift it up and over her head, and then he tossed it aside, coming back to admire her in the black lacy underwear she'd worn in the hope of turning him on.

It seemed to work. He ran his fingers over the tops of her breasts, propped up in the lacy demi-cups, his breaths coming fast, his mouth hot as it claimed hers again. As his tongue toyed with hers, she felt his hands slip around her back, and then he'd released her bra and tossed that aside too.

His hands found her breasts, his palms warm, and he groaned as he pressed her back against the glass. It was cold and she gasped, but all he did was deepen the kiss, and then his mouth left hers and he was kissing her neck, her collarbone, and down to her breasts, where he closed his mouth over a nipple.

She tipped her head back on the glass, sighing her approval as he licked and sucked, teasing both nipples to tight peaks. Then he dropped to his knees, taking the elastic of her panties in his fingers, and he pulled them down her legs and held her while she stepped out of them. Without further ado, he leaned forward and slid his tongue down her mound and into her folds.

Crying out with pleasure, she tightened her fingers in his hair, feeling wicked at the thought that someone down in the street could look up and see her pressed up against the window, naked. But she didn't care. The decadence of it all made her feel alive, and she felt herself smiling, enjoying the sheer pleasure of being here, being with him.

Cameron slid his fingers down into her, easily enough that she knew she was wet and swollen for him. His thumb circled over her clit as he explored with his other fingers, sliding them inside her. She clamped her teeth on her bottom lip as he collected some of her moisture and slid a finger up to tease the tight muscle at the back.

"Oh Jesus." She moaned, her legs trembling, as he stroked and sucked, teasing her nearer and nearer to the edge. Please God, don't let her knees give way.

As if conscious of her fear, Cameron removed his fingers and pushed up to face her, then quickly shed the rest of his clothes before applying a condom. Within seconds he was back, holding her in his arms, and then he lifted her and pressed her up against the glass.

She squealed. "You'll drop me!"

"I won't. Just relax."

She scrunched up her eyes, knowing she was too heavy. "I'm twenty pounds heavier than I was at eighteen."

He laughed as he guided the tip of his erection beneath her. "You're still tiny, though." He pushed forward a little, sliding into her folds, then stopped and kissed her. "Relax," he murmured.

"Don't you want to make love on a nice soft bed?" she asked faintly.

"Nope." He moved his head back to look at her, and kept his eyes on hers as he slid into her.

Her head tipped back onto the glass again. "Oh my God…"

"Holy shit, you're wet. Why did you think you'd ever need lube?"

"Cam…"

"I'm going to fuck you senseless. I hope you're ready."

This was a dream. A hot, raunchy dream, and she was going to wake up at home all feverish and sticking to the bedclothes.

But the cold glass on her back, the heat of his mouth, and the hardness of him inside her told her it was all too real, and he wasn't going to let her go until he'd taken what he wanted from her.

Crushing his lips to hers, he thrust inside her, and she wrapped her legs around his waist and let him take her, carried away on a blissful sea of pleasure. She was sure they'd never done anything as sexy as this even when they were young, although then she remembered previous lovemaking sessions when he'd tied her up and teased her to several orgasms over the space of a few hours, or when he'd brought home a variety of vibrators that he'd then proceeded to try out on her. He'd always been like this, hot and hungry, and the years had changed nothing, she thought. He was as gorgeous as the day she'd met him, maybe even more so, with all his years of experience and maturity to add to his innate sexiness.

He lifted his head and studied her, a wry look on his face. "You're not going to relax up there, are you?"

"I'm getting there," she protested, but he chuckled and lifted her off the glass. "You said you weren't going to fuck me on the table," she teased as he took her over to the large wooden dining table.

"I said I wasn't yesterday," he corrected. "Today, I'm in the mood." He lowered her until she rested on the edge, and she leaned back on her hands, giving a little gasp at the coolness of the wood.

"It's cold."

"Don't care," he said, and he thrust forward, hard.

She moaned and fell back onto her elbows, and he started to thrust properly, sliding easily through her moist folds, his hips meeting the back of her thighs with a sharp slap. It was pointless to protest, not that she wanted to anyway, because this was hot as hell, and she was so turned on she could already feel the orgasm approaching as he leaned over her, grinding against her with each thrust.

"Oh jeez," she whispered, lifting her arms above her head and stretching out beneath him as she felt the arrival of a climax she was sure was going to send her into a coma.

"Fuck yeah," he said, and he pounded into her as she came and cried out with the intensity of it, the sweet, sharp clenches deep inside, the pleasure that was like nothing else in the world, so beautiful and bittersweet, the pulses so fast and hard and tight it was almost painful. Cameron rode her through it, his skin slick with sweat, sliding against hers, and then, as her own body released her, he came, turning to rock beneath her fingers, his muscles tightening, hips jerking, teeth grinding, as he pushed forward hard.

"Holy shit." He finished with a groan, leaning over her on both hands, his chest heaving. "Christ. Did I hurt you?"

She laughed. "No. Although I think you might have speared me to the table."

"I'm so sorry."

"Don't be." She pulled him down for a long, lingering kiss. "Mmm. It was… mmm… heavenly."

He chuckled and pushed up, withdrew and disposed of the condom, then helped her up from the table. Bending, he picked her up and carried her through to the bedroom, and laid her carefully on the bed. Climbing on with her, he tugged the duvet over them and pulled her into his arms.

"I'm sorry," he said again. "I was a bit rough. I don't know what came over me."

She looked up into his eyes, which appeared black in the semi-darkness, with a glint of silver from the moon that shone through the open curtains. "I thought I'd never experience passion like that again," she whispered, tracing her fingers over his lips. "I didn't think I'd ever make love to another man."

"It would have been a crime." He kissed her, taking his time to move his lips across hers slowly, sliding his hands down her back.

Noelle let him, wallowing in the sexual satisfaction, but inside she couldn't deny a touch of sadness. Soon, he would be leaving New Zealand, and then she'd have to return to her life in the Bay of Islands. It was wonderful, and she wasn't complaining. But she would miss this, now she knew what it could be like. She knew she would be lying awake late into the night, dreaming about Cameron and his dark eyes and his passion until the end of her days.

And suddenly, the epithet of it being better to have loved and lost than never to have loved at all didn't seem quite so true. How was she going to cope when he got on that plane? When he left her life—this time for good?

Chapter Nineteen

The next morning, they said goodbye to Marcus and Rebecca, who were taking a taxi for the ferry across the Cook Strait to Picton to begin their journey south, promising to keep in touch all the way.

Cameron and Noelle headed out to Wellington airport, where they caught a flight to Rotorua and collected a hire car. As they drove into what had been nicknamed 'The Sulphur City', the distinct smell of rotten eggs soon permeated the vehicle.

"Wasn't me," Cameron told her, making her laugh.

"You get used to it," she advised.

Cameron wasn't so sure, but true enough, after a few hours it no longer seemed quite as odious, and the place was so interesting it was worth the occasional unpleasant whiff that drifted their way. They took a tour around the thermal park, and Noelle told him all about the Ring of Fire, the area in the Pacific basin where many earthquakes and volcanic eruptions occurred.

"It has 452 volcanoes," she told him as they walked around the thermal reserve, where the water bubbled in pools as if it were in a pot on the stove. "About ninety percent of all the world's earthquakes occur along the Ring."

He knew a fair amount about geology, but most of his work had been carried out in the Atlantic, and he hadn't realized quite how active New Zealand was. "Jesus." He stepped back as the nearby geyser erupted, spraying water what must have been forty feet in the air. "Do you worry about being caught in an earthquake or a volcanic eruption?"

"Not so much in the Northland." She led him past bubbling pools of mud that spat occasionally at passing visitors. "We veer away from the Ring up there. You'll see lots of flat-topped volcanoes. The last one erupted about two thousand years ago, I think. We very rarely have earthquakes up there, not like in Wellington or Christchurch."

"You know a lot about your country," he said as they carried on around the colorful hot lakes. "I tend to think of you as English still, but I suppose you consider yourself a New Zealander?"

"I got my citizenship a long time ago, so yes, I suppose I do think of myself as a Kiwi."

"You have a Kiwi accent."

"Do I?"

"You say 'yis' not yes. 'Pin' not pen. And your voice goes up at the end of sentences."

She smiled. "You still sound like a Cockney."

"Sarf London boy, ain't I?" He grinned, but the conversation reminded him that she'd come a long way from the woman he'd met all those years ago. Then she'd been a city girl, at home with the buses and the Tube and black cabs, smart and sassy, loving the music of the early eighties, Culture Club and Wham! and Duran Duran, going to clubs, living the high life. Now she lived in a small town and filled her days with gardening and watching amateur theater productions and having barbecues with her families. Life couldn't be more different for her.

"Do you miss it?" he asked as they began to head back to the car. "The shows and concerts. The shopping. I imagine it's not quite the same in Auckland or Wellington."

"Lots of bands come here, although I can't remember the last time I went to a concert," she admitted. "Hugh wasn't really into music."

Cameron didn't say anything, but he thought back to when they would have the radio on all day and night, when music was all that seemed to matter. "Do you still listen to any?"

"Oh yes. Dominic bought me a record player so I've gone back to vinyl, and I tend to play records in the evenings and read rather than watch TV now I'm on my own." She looked away.

He squeezed her hand. "Sorry. Didn't mean to make you sad."

"It's okay." She gave him a small smile. "It's strange how you change when you're with a partner though, isn't it? You mold yourself to each other, changing in imperceptible ways to make yourself fit. Since he died, I've sort of relaxed back into my own shape in many ways. Hugh didn't like spicy food, but I cook Mexican and Indian meals all the time now. He didn't mind historical movies, but he wasn't keen on science fiction and fantasy or anything that wasn't 'real'. I spent the first few months after he died losing myself in all the movies and series I'd wanted to see for years."

She glanced at him then. "You're thinking that it doesn't sound as if we had much in common," she said, somewhat defensively.

"Not at all," he replied, although it had seemed strange to him that she should have married someone who didn't like the same music or movies, when those things had been so important to her.

"He was different," she said. "That's all."

"Than what?"

"Than you."

He stopped walking, and she stopped too and turned to face him.

"That surprises you?" she asked. "That I chose him because he was different?"

He didn't say anything.

"I've hurt your feelings," she said softly, moving closer to him. "Sweetheart, I don't mean that I wanted someone different because I wanted to forget you. I didn't want to look for someone who was like you because I knew I'd never find someone to match up to you." She kissed his cheek. "It's like when you buy a custard doughnut from a baker's, and it's the best custard doughnut you've ever had, so you have one every day for weeks. And then when you move to another town, you don't want to try their baker's doughnuts because you know they're never going to be as good, so you get apple pie instead. The apple pie is great, but it means you'll never spoil the memory of that doughnut."

He slid his arms around her waist and kissed her. Her arms rose around his neck, and it turned into a lingering kiss that left him filled with longing.

"Did that make sense?" she asked when he finally moved back.

"Only you could compare me to a custard doughnut," he said, his voice husky with emotion. His reply was glib, but her sentiment had touched him more than she'd ever know. And anyway, hadn't he done the same? They'd both married very different people so they wouldn't be reminded of what they'd lost.

"Come on." She took his hand and led him back to the car. "Let's head on to Matamata. I'm really looking forward to the tour!"

So they got back in the car and headed up the State Highway toward the home of Hobbiton. Cameron had booked them on a special evening banquet tour, so they had time to check in at the farm-stay they'd chosen for the night first and drop off their bags before heading out to the movie set.

The tour turned out to be amazing, a trek through the twelve-acre site of the Shire at dusk, their guide relating many stories about the filming of the trilogy as well as tales about the original Tolkien stories that Cameron loved. They ended up at the Green Dragon Inn where they sat with their fellow travelers around a long dining table and had a banquet fit for Hobbits before they walked back through the Shire with hand-held lanterns, amazed by the stunning views of the Hobbit Holes lit up in the darkness.

It was an awesome experience he would never forget, made even more special by the presence of Noelle at his side. As they made their way back to the farm-stay, he thought what a magical adventure this trip to New Zealand had been. He'd never have been able to predict that this could have happened.

They arrived at the farm-stay, let themselves into their cute and cozy room, and Noelle fell back onto the bed, stretching out with a long sigh.

"What an amazing evening," she said. "That was a night to remember, wasn't it?"

Cameron climbed onto the bed beside her, slid an arm around her waist, and rolled onto his back, bringing her on top of him. "It was. I'll never forget it."

She looked down at him, her brow flickering with a frown as she brushed the back of her fingers across his cheek. "You've become such a serious man," she murmured. "I remember you as being so lighthearted and full of fun."

"Life has a way of doing that to you." He held her tightly, wishing the night would last forever, and that the two of them could stay like this, entwined around each other, kissing and making love for the rest of eternity.

"Do you wish you hadn't come here?" she whispered.

His eyebrows rose. "Of course not. It's been amazing."

"You don't regret meeting me after all this time?"

"Why would I do that?"

"Because we'll have to part all over again. And it's going to be hard." Her eyes shone, suggesting tears weren't far from the surface. She wasn't finding this easy. She was going to have as much trouble as he was when it was time for him to leave.

"Don't let's think about that now," he said, and he slid a hand into her hair and brought her head down to kiss her.

She let him, her mouth slanting across his, but after a minute or two she lifted her head again to look at him. "You've set me free," she said. "You know that, right? I know it means it'll be hard to part, but I'm glad we met. You've reminded me how wonderful it can be to be in love, with all the heat and heart of youth."

He looked up into her wide green eyes, his heart racing. Was she saying she loved him still? He didn't want to ask, and he didn't dare to hope, but her words warmed him all the way through.

She undid the button at the top of his jeans and slid down his zipper. Then, shifting on the bed, she moved off him, kissing down his chest to where his erection strained toward her through the fabric of his boxers. Carefully, she pushed down the elastic, releasing him, and he closed his eyes and held his breath as she kissed along the trail of hair leading from his navel and then covered the tip of his erection with her mouth.

Ohhh jeez, that felt amazing. He lifted his arms above his head and just let her kiss him for a while, swelling in her mouth as she traced the tip of her tongue across the top, then took him deep into her mouth and sucked. She stroked him firmly at the same time, and he opened his eyes and watched the shadows playing across the ceiling, sighs escaping his lips as she teased him with the brush of her soft tongue.

"You should stop there," he murmured as pleasure stirred in his belly, causing muscles deep inside to tighten. But she didn't, murmuring her approval instead, taking him even deeper in her mouth, and he couldn't stand it any longer. He gave in and let her coax him to a climax, burying a hand in her hair, groaning as he came, and gasping as she swallowed him down.

"Fuck," he said out loud, lifting his hands and pressing them into his eyes. "*Ohhh*.... Holy fuck."

She moved up the bed to kiss his cheek. "I haven't done that in a while."

"And yet you could still win an Olympic Gold."

They both laughed. "You taste nice," she whispered, nuzzling his ear.

"And you're still a minx. I was going to screw you senseless tonight."

"Plenty of time for that later."

"Are you trying to give me a heart attack? I am fifty-four."

She snorted. "Like that's made any difference. You're still as insatiable as ever."

He grinned and rolled onto his side to face her, sliding a hand up her skirt. "Not as insatiable as you, I think."

"I'm sex-starved. I'm like a woman in a desert, dying of thirst... oh!" Her lips parted in a gasp as he lifted the elastic of her panties and slipped his fingers down into her. "Mmm."

"Oh yeah." He was pleased to find her wet and swollen, glad that she hadn't yet had need of the lube she'd brought with her. He slid two fingers deep inside her, coating them with her moisture, then brought them up to circle over her clit. She moaned and he kissed her, knowing it wouldn't be long before she came. Some things never changed, he thought, stroking her firmly the way he'd learned to do all those years ago, and feeling the answering tension build in her muscles.

"Cameron..." she whispered, and he kissed her more deeply, his fingers sliding through her slippery folds, and then she came, her hips jerking against his hand as he pressed down on her clit. Fierce joy engulfed him at the thought that he'd given her pleasure, and he watched as the aftershocks of her orgasm rippled through her, listening to her little sighs, feeling the rock of her hips against his hand as her body gradually calmed.

When she'd done, he withdrew his hand and she rolled toward him, murmuring, "Mmm. What a lovely way to end the evening."

He wrapped his arms around her, looking over her shoulder at the moon outside, thinking how beautiful the night had been as they'd walked through the Shire, holding hands.

He didn't want to let her go.

And, in fact, he wasn't going to.

The realization came to him so suddenly that his heart skipped a beat. He didn't have to let her go. There was one option.

"Let's get in bed," she said, and he nodded, rising with her and undressing. Inside, his mind was a whirl with this new idea. He wanted to blurt it out to her, to tell her what he was thinking, but he made himself keep quiet. He'd plan it first, and only then would he tell her what was on his mind. Until then, he'd hold her close, and make the most of every minute, just in case it didn't work out.

Chapter Twenty

The next day, they left after breakfast, Noelle feeling some sadness at leaving the Shire behind. They passed through the beautiful town of Cambridge, the self-named "town of trees and champions", which made Cameron smile, and then on past Hamilton and up to Auckland.

He'd booked them into a top hotel in the Central Business District overlooking the City of Sails. Their luxury suite was situated in the corner of the building and therefore had a magnificent view of the private marina with its million-dollar yachts. She walked into the living room with its two long sofas, its hand-carved oak dining table that could seat eight, and its huge bedroom, and wondered how much it had cost him.

"Do you always stay in the most expensive suite?" she asked as the porter withdrew, closing the door behind him.

"No. So it's a treat for me, too." He walked over to the floor-to-ceiling windows to look down at the marina.

Noelle studied him, thinking how handsome he was with the sunlight falling across him, making his gray hair shine, highlighting his strong features, his sensual mouth. She doubted that he ever stayed in the cheapest rooms, but he'd obviously booked the top suites during their holiday because he wanted to impress her.

He turned to look at her and smiled as he saw her watching him. "Come on. We've got a busy day and lots to do!"

They caught a quick lunch in a nearby café, then spent a few hours exploring the shops. When they'd had enough, they returned to the hotel, where Noelle discovered that he'd booked them a luxury couples' treatment in the spa. Hugh had never been interested in anything like that, so she was excited to go down to the spa with Cameron. In a warm room lit with candles, they were led to two massage tables, where they undressed and lay on their fronts, covered with towels. A special aromatic syrup was applied to their skin, which was then exfoliated with a Moroccan terracotta pumice stone that left her glowing. Finally they had a full body massage that had her almost dozing off by the time every last ounce of tension had dissipated.

But then it was time for dinner, and they spent a couple of hours over their meal. They treated themselves to seared scallops, sugar-cured kingfish with wasabi, Hawkes Bay lamb rump with ricotta gnocchi, and an amazing Tahitian vanilla creme dessert that had Noelle sighing with every spoonful.

Finally they took a coffee out onto the balcony, overlooking the marina. It was now mid-November, heading toward summer, the evenings holding a touch of a chill as the hour grew late and the sun dipped below the horizon. Noelle wrapped a pashmina around her shoulders, and they sat there for a long time, letting their dinner go down as they talked about the past and the present, discussing their families, their jobs, and life in general.

By the time they returned to their room, she was more than ready to extend what had been a sensual day in every way around by letting Cameron undress her slowly and slide his hands over her soft, still-glowing skin. She waited for him to turn up the dial, to let his passion overwhelm them both the way it had every time they'd made love so far, but this time he seemed keen to take it slow, and once they were both naked he slid beneath the covers with her and spent a long while touching her and kissing her, until she was ready to beg him to take her.

He moved on top of her, donned a condom, and eased into her, then lowered down and continued to kiss her as he moved, taking his time.

"Mmm." She stroked her hands over his shoulders and down his chest, feeling as if she were in a dream world. "You drive me crazy, you know that?"

"And you me." He kissed her, his tongue playing with hers, still moving slowly inside her. "Come with me."

"Mmm, yes please. This feels amazing."

"No." He stopped moving and looked into her eyes. "Come with me to England."

She blinked a few times, her brain struggling to catch up. "What?"

He began to move again, and kissed around to her ear. "I'm not ready to give you up yet. You said you hadn't been back to England since you moved here. Let's extend our holiday another few weeks. Come back and spend some time there with me. You can meet my kids, and we'll see some of the sights we used to love, go to the theater… whatever you want."

She let him kiss her, her body still responding to his touch, even though her mind was elsewhere, churning over his words.

He didn't say anything more, obviously realizing she needed to think about it, and his thrusts grew more insistent, telling her he wasn't far from coming. She knew he'd asked her in bed on purpose, thinking that she'd be so caught up in the moment that she'd agree without thinking. She didn't, though, unable to avoid a tug of disappointment. Part of her had secretly hoped that this short trip through New Zealand would have shown him how wonderful the country was, and that he might, just might, consider moving there to be with her. But now she realized how foolish she'd been. His job, his life, was in London and elsewhere in the world. New Zealand was so far from everywhere. It was the last place he'd ever want to live permanently.

"Ah, Noelle… Tell me you'll always be my girl." He crushed his lips to hers, plunging his tongue into her mouth.

She couldn't reply, couldn't even think as he thrust hard, driving them both closer to a climax, and she pushed all thoughts from her mind and gave in to her body's urge to respond, tightening around him and crying out. They came together, and she moaned his name, feeling his skin slick beneath her hands, enjoying the movement of his muscles as his hips gave a few final jerks.

When he'd done, he lifted off her, disposed of the condom, moved beside her, and took her into his arms.

She curled up against him, her brain starting to reboot now the physical pleasure had passed.

He didn't want to let her go. Even after all this time, his feelings were still strong for her.

And hers were for him. She couldn't deny it. Once she'd met Hugh and found a different kind of love, she'd assumed that what she thought she felt for Cameron had been mostly in the mind, or born out of the passion of youth. Now she knew she'd been wrong. Her feelings for him were the same as they had been back then—fierce and strong, a love completely different from that she'd felt for the kind, quiet Hugh. She'd given Hugh five children, had stood by his side and looked after him, had run his house, and supported him until the day he was taken from her. She'd loved him absolutely. But her feelings for Cameron were completely different.

But how was she to weigh those feelings against what he'd asked of her?

"I can't let you go," he murmured in the semi-darkness. "Not yet. I'm not ready."

"Will you ever be ready?"

"I don't know."

She placed a hand on his chest, watching it rise and fall, feeling the beat of his heart beneath her palm. When the kids were young, she and Hugh had bought them a dog, a beautiful Labrador called Bessie, who'd lived to the ripe old age of fourteen. Noelle had loved the dog with all her heart, and she'd cried buckets when Bessie died. The kids had been teenagers by then, and they'd suggested she get another dog, but she'd been hesitant to commit her heart again, afraid of the power of grief.

Perhaps it was terrible to compare one's husband to a dog, but she felt much the same way about her love life. She'd loved Hugh completely, and when he'd died so abruptly she'd been devastated. She'd held it together for her kids, but even though over the last two years she'd felt sad at the thought that she might never lie with another man again, part of her had been relieved that she wouldn't have to commit her heart, and risk breaking it again.

It was going to break anyway when she and Cameron finally parted. And part they would, because whatever he thought, she was never going to leave her family, and he was never going to move to New Zealand—it was clear to her that he would never consider it. So what was the point in dragging this out? Why not part now and have done with it?

His chest rose and fell, rose and fell; his heart beat against her palm. She closed her eyes, feeling such a mixture of emotions that it made her stomach churn—pleasure, pain, hope, fear. She was too old to take this kind of risk. Too old to fall in love, to have hopes, to feel dizzy with love, to have the sort of longing that made you sigh when you thought about the other person.

And yet here she was, feeling all those things.

"Say something," he said. "Have I upset you?"

"No."

"You're sure?"

She hesitated, then pushed herself up to look at him. "I feel a bit… manipulated, I suppose. You told me while we were making love—you can't tell me you weren't hoping that would be influential."

He gave her a boyish, sheepish smile. "Maybe."

"You know it doesn't make sense."

"None of it makes sense." He ran a hand slowly down her back. "Seeing you, being with you, after all this time… Would it have been better for us if I'd turned around at the ball and walked the other way? It would have been simpler. Would it have made me happier? Hell, no. I'd have been moping around driving Marcus and Rebecca nuts, thinking of you being somewhere in the country, there but out of my reach."

He lifted her hand where it lay on his chest and kissed her fingers. "I'm glad we got together. It's been an amazing few days. But it's not enough. Maybe in a few weeks, it will be. Maybe it won't. Who knows?"

"So, what? You're hoping that I'll change my mind and say I'll stay in England?"

He shrugged.

"It's not going to happen, Cam. Don't get your hopes up."

He met her gaze, and some of the light died in his eyes. "I know," he said quietly. "And I don't expect you to leave your family. But who can say what will happen? Maybe we'll decide we're done and we'll keep in touch on Facebook and by email. Perhaps we'll end up calling a few times a week. I could visit a couple of times a year; you could come to London."

"A long-distance relationship?" Her brow furrowed.

"Would it be so terrible? I know I'm never going to get married again. I don't know if it's on the cards for you, but I have a feeling it would have to be someone very special. So what, we're going to stay single for the rest of our lives? Do you really mean never to have sex again as long as you live?"

She pursed her lips. It wasn't an attractive thought. "So you're saying I'll be your bit of skirt in New Zealand? The one you see when you're in the southern hemisphere?" She raised her eyebrows at his frown. "Come on, you've practically told me you have a girl in every port."

"It's not like that."

"So you'd want us to be exclusive?"

"Yes."

That surprised her. He was suggesting a real long-distance relationship. That they have some sort of commitment and see each other a few times a year.

They studied each other for a long while.

"I don't think I could afford to fly to the UK every year," she said.

"I'd pay for you to fly as often as you could. Of course I would. Don't let that be the reason you say no."

It wasn't the worst idea in the world, she thought. Her life would continue much the same, focused around her friends and family. And then every now and again she'd meet up with him, either in New Zealand or in England, or maybe somewhere in between, and they'd spend some time together, and share a bed, until the time came when one of them said they'd had enough, or they were too old to travel.

And then what? At some point she was going to have to say goodbye to him forever. She couldn't help but think that it was inevitable that he was going to break her heart.

But maybe that was a childish thought. They were grownups now, mature adults who enjoyed each other's company. He hadn't said he loved her in so many words, but childish declarations of passion had no place in the real world, when they had commitments and responsibilities.

So what sort of wise woman did she want to be? The sort who took the well-lit road through the forest, avoiding the paths that might have led either to fortune or to disaster, in favor of a safe, secure route through life? Or a woman who took risks, who lived for today, who followed her heart and squeezed the most out of every minute?

Cameron wasn't saying that he just wanted her for sex, or that he would sleep with other women when they weren't together. He wanted to be with her, he wanted her to be his, and while it wasn't as romantic as a heartfelt declaration of love and a promise that he would be at her side for the rest of his life, this was the only way he could think of to make this work.

"Can I think about it?" she whispered.

"Of course. Now turn over, and we'll snuggle up and get some sleep."

She did so, feeling him move up close to her, his chest against her back, his arm snaking around her waist.

"Sleep tight, sweetheart," he said, kissing her ear.

But it would be a long, long while before she finally closed her eyes.

Chapter Twenty-One

It took nearly four hours for them to drive from Auckland back to Kerikeri, and all the way Cameron worried he'd pushed his luck too far.

Noelle chatted to him and pointed out sights along the way, but she was quiet, and he knew she was thinking about his suggestion of the night before.

He felt a sense of desperation settle over him the nearer they got to her home. Part of him had hoped that she would fling her arms around his neck and say of course she would go with him, and wasn't it wonderful of him to have asked her? But she hadn't. And now he was worried she was going to say no. If she did, he would soon be saying goodbye to her for good. He felt almost queasy with the mixture of anger, frustration, and terror that churned in his stomach. How could he get on the plane and fly off, knowing he'd found her and lost her again?

Well, he'd have to. He had to accept that for once he had no control over his own life, and he'd have to let Fate take its course.

He fought the urge to either get down on his knees and beg or handcuff her to him and drag her onto the plane. He couldn't imagine either of those scenarios ending well.

They approached the roundabout leading to the turnoff to her road, and he indicated and steered the car around. "Not far now," he said, trying to sound positive. "Thank you for coming with me to Wellington. I've had a great time."

"Me too."

"You have a wonderful country. I'm glad I got to share it for a while."

She held out her hand, and he rested his on top, closing his fingers around hers.

"I'm staying in the hotel on the edge of town tonight," he said. "I've already booked it. I didn't want you to have to worry about whether I was expecting to stay at your home."

"That's very thoughtful, Cam."

"I try." He smiled.

She brushed her thumb over the back of his hand. "I've been thinking a lot about what you said."

"I know." He lifted her hand and kissed her knuckles. "I'm sorry I've put you in that position."

"It's okay. I mean, it's not an easy decision, but I realized that I'm touched—thrilled—that you want to see me again. That you don't want to get on the plane and leave."

"Jesus, Noelle, of course I don't. I've just found you again! Forever would be too soon to say goodbye." He glanced at her and saw her eyes glisten. "Aw. Too much?"

She sniffed. "No. Keep saying nice things."

He smiled again. "I'm crazy about you. I never stopped feeling that way, I've realized. I just put my feelings on hold. But I never stopped loving you."

"L-loving me?"

He released her hand to indicate as her drive approached, turned onto the road, and headed for the house. "Yes, of course. I said that last night." He glanced at her. "Didn't I?"

She gave a little shake of her head.

He gritted his teeth. Fucking idiot. He'd been saying it in his head all the time he'd been making love to her.

He pulled up outside her house, put on the handbrake, turned off the engine, and unclipped his seatbelt. Then he faced her and took her hand in his. "I love you. I always have, and I suspect I always will. I meant to say it last night, and I can't believe I didn't. I'm sorry. I'm an imbecile. Please forgive me."

She swallowed hard. Her face had paled. "We've been together three days. How can you talk about love with such surety?"

He frowned. "Don't talk to me as if I'm someone else. We've not known each other three days. I've held you in my heart for over thirty years." His voice came out harsher than he'd meant, and he cleared his throat. He desperately wanted her to understand. "Nothing's changed. I thought it would have, and it seems crazy that it hasn't, but it's the truth. I don't understand it. I know you're different now, you've been married, loved someone else, had a family. You're a businesswoman, and you have very different interests. We're not the same people we were back then. And yet, whatever it is that resides in me—whether you call it a soul, a spark, or something else—it recognized you, and what it feels for you is as strong as it's ever been."

He lifted her chin with his hand to look into her eyes. "In fact, maybe it's stronger, because with it comes the wisdom of age and the knowledge that love isn't a flimsy trick of the light or sleight of hand. It's not an arrow to the heart or a flare of hormones. It's more than that, isn't it? It's trust and companionship, and desire. I feel all those things for you. I want to be with you. I want to make love to you. I want to hold you in my arms at night. If that's not love, then I have no idea what is."

He was talking too much. Marcus called it his auto-mouth syndrome, and said it was part of Cameron's conviction that he could talk anyone into anything providing he didn't give them enough space to think about the drawbacks. He didn't want to talk Noelle into coming with him. He wanted her to make that decision on her own.

Despair began to bloom inside him, and he closed his eyes.

"The answer's yes," she said.

He waited a heartbeat, then opened his eyes again. "What?"

"Yes. I'll come to England with you for a week or two, providing I can find someone to cover me at the shop."

His jaw dropped as he gasped, and he pulled her toward him.

She put a hand on his chest. "It's temporary. You get that, right? I won't be turning around after a week and declaring that I'm staying."

"I know." He was pretty certain she wouldn't, but then stranger things had happened at sea, and he was so happy that he didn't have to say goodbye that he was willing to wait and see what Fate had planned for him later. "Come here." He wrapped his arms around her and kissed her, his heart swelling at the feel of her lips beneath his. He hadn't lost her. He had time to figure things out, to show her how much he loved her, and maybe convince her that they couldn't be apart. That was all he wanted.

*

Noelle spent the next two days in a whirl, trying to get everything organized for her time away.

Roberta had hired a new local girl called Marama to help in the café, which released an excited Cathy to run the shop. Noelle spent most of

Sunday going through the books with her, making sure she knew the ins and outs of ordering and delivery, and how to organize the finances.

"I'll email every day," Noelle told her nervously, "and I'll always be available on FaceTime if you need to talk—you can call me any time."

"Will you stop worrying?" Cathy scolded. "Go away and have an amazing time with Mr. Smart and Sexy."

Noelle blushed. "You think I'm doing the right thing?"

"Of course you're doing the right thing. What woman in her right mind would say no to Cameron Taylor? Make the most of it, sweetheart. Life's far too short to umm and aah over opportunities like this."

She was right, Noelle thought, and the tension that had pervaded her seemed to lift then, as she mused that all she was doing was having an amazing holiday for two weeks. Cameron was right—they'd visit their teenage haunts, and she'd be able to catch up with some old friends and family. And maybe he was right about their relationship. They were older and more mature. It didn't have to be about ultimatums and declarations of all or nothing. Anything less than one-hundred percent commitment didn't automatically mean failure. It didn't have to be the end of the world every time one of them got on a plane. She just had to accept that she wasn't living a fairytale. If she wanted to stay in touch with him, it was her choice and she was in control.

Cameron had booked their flight out for Tuesday afternoon, so she spent most of Monday nipping around saying goodbye to everyone, especially her kids. They all seemed excited for her, even Phoebe, who gave her a big hug and said of course she should go, and she should make sure she had a great time and didn't think about them at all. Noelle knew she'd never manage that, but she appreciated her daughter's words, and she was glad that Phoebe seemed reconciled to the fact that her mother was dating again.

Tuesday morning came all too soon, and by ten a.m. Cameron was out the front in the hire car waiting for her. She'd taken the previous afternoon to pack, and he helped her put her suitcase in the car, and it was time to set off for the airport.

They flew to Auckland, where he'd booked them First Class seats to London via Singapore. She'd never flown First Class before, and thought she could very easily get used to the comfortable chairs that converted into a bed, the exquisite food, and the complimentary champagne.

She felt a strange mixture of emotions as the plane took off. She went to Auckland often enough that she was used to staying away from home, but it was odd to be leaving the country. She'd been on holiday many times over the years, mainly to one of the Pacific Islands, or occasionally to Australia, but Europe was over twenty-four hours away, and Hugh had never had a burning passion to go there, so they'd never been. Maybe if she'd had brothers and sisters over there, she thought as New Zealand disappeared behind her, she would have felt more of a need to return to England. Deep down, though, she was sure part of her reason for staying away was because she'd been afraid that if she went back, she'd feel drawn to see Cameron again, and then she would never have been able to leave.

"Penny for them," he asked, squeezing her hand where it rested on his thigh.

"Just thinking that I haven't been back for so long," she said, giving him a smile. "I wonder how much the country has changed."

"Some, I would imagine. London's always been multicultural, but it's even more so now."

"I can't wait to see Subaqueous," she said. He'd promised her he'd show her around the main office.

"And I can't wait to show you my pride and joy."

"You must let me know if you have to work," she told him. "I don't expect you to be at my side twenty-four-seven."

"Absolutely I'm going to be glued to you. You'll be sick of the sight of me by the time you go." He grinned at her.

She smiled back, although she felt a flutter of nerves. She would be meeting his children, and maybe even his ex-wife, Lara. That would be weird. Were his kids likely to be hostile? Was Lara?

"Have you ever mentioned me to your ex?" she asked.

He glanced at her. "To Lara?"

"Yes."

"She knows about you, yes."

"What have you told her?"

He gave her an amused look. "I'm not telling you."

"Why?" Now she was intrigued.

"I think your head's big enough as it is with all the compliments I've been giving you. Now, I was thinking about where we should go once we're there. Any shows you want to see?"

She let him talk on about the places he wanted to take her while she was there, but inside she pondered on what he might have said to Lara. Perhaps he'd mentioned her in passing, the way you sometimes do when talking to your partner about previous girlfriends and boyfriends. *Noelle was a girl I met while I was at uni. We went out for a while before she had to move to New Zealand.* Perhaps it had been as simple as that.

Sometimes, she wondered whether Hugh had ever thought about Cameron. When she'd first started dating Hugh, she'd told him straight up that she'd been in love with a man back in England, but that she'd had to leave him to come to New Zealand. She'd gotten upset as she told him, and had shed a few tears. Hugh had said he understood, and that he would never try to replace Cameron in her heart, but that he hoped she would grow to love him in her own way.

Had he ever been jealous? He'd certainly never said anything that made her think he was. He'd seemed to accept that her first love was in her past, and had been unconcerned about whether he matched up to him.

"Don't be sad," Cameron said, squeezing her fingers.

"I'm sorry. I won't, I promise." She raised his hand and kissed it. She wasn't going to think about Hugh. It wasn't fair to him, and it wasn't fair to Cameron. She was going to enjoy herself, and make the most of this amazing opportunity to travel, to see her old home, and to be with the man who still made her heart race.

Chapter Twenty-Two

Noelle had thought that the two weeks in London would fly by, but to her surprise time seemed to slow as soon as the plane set down its wheels at Heathrow. It was probably because they were so busy, she thought. At the end of each day she wrote an email to Cathy or her kids, and she was always surprised when she recounted all the things they'd managed to cram into one day.

Cameron rented a two-bedroomed apartment in a quiet area in Shoreditch, on the twenty-fifth floor of a building, with panoramic views across the city. They'd spent a lot of time in Shoreditch when they were first together, and it still felt young, vibrant, and artsy, full of shops selling hand-carved spoons and handmade soaps, artisan coffee shops and noodle bars.

The apartment had herringbone flooring, honed marble in the *en suite* bathroom, a top-of-the-range kitchen, and an amazing sky-garden. It was smart and swish and must have cost him a fortune, but she had the feeling he didn't spend much time there. And sure enough, they went out early most days and didn't return until late.

They went to Westminster Abbey and St. Paul's Cathedral, to the V&A and the National Gallery and the British Museum, and to places that hadn't existed when she lived there, like the Millennium Wheel and the reconstruction of Shakespeare's Globe.

They ate out in cafés and burger joints and expensive restaurants, and they went to shows and movies and met old friends and made new ones.

She'd thought that, knowing he was a workaholic, he might have to work more, but it seemed that for two weeks he hardly left her side. He was always touching her, holding her hand, his arm around her shoulders, or a hand in the small of her back, possessive, she thought, telling everyone they met that although he was introducing her as his friend, their relationship was much more than that. The rare time they spent a few hours apart, when she met up with some old school friends and he called into work for a few hours, he texted her half-a-dozen times, as if he couldn't bear to be out of contact with her.

She loved the days, and she knew she'd never forget the amazing times they had, but it was the nights that were the most magical. It was nearly the end of November now, and it seemed to rain a lot at night, hammering on the windows and somehow cutting them off from the rest of the world. Each night they took a drink to bed, a glass of wine or a tumbler of whisky, and lay there with the curtains open, looking out over the city.

Most nights they made love, Cameron always insatiable, hungering for her. Sometimes it was fast and furious, or erotic in a way she'd never thought to experience again, so much more than married-style fumbling beneath the bedclothes. He wanted her everywhere and every way, no different from the young man who'd consumed her every waking moment back when she was eighteen. She grew used to the delicious ache in her muscles that followed a lovemaking session, and stopped feeling so self-conscious or embarrassed about her body, because he took such delight in it.

In the second week she met his children, an experience that was both pleasant and somehow sad, as it made her think about what her children would have looked like if Cameron had been the father. She loved her kids with all her heart and she wouldn't change a thing, but it was strange to be faced with alternate realities, and to wonder what might have been.

Josh she met at a restaurant with his girlfriend. He looked very like Cameron, tall and handsome, with his father's charm and natural ability to put people at ease. They had lunch while Josh told them about the new job he had lined up working at one of the top restaurants in London, and his girlfriend talked about her career in finance. It soon became apparent to Noelle that Josh led his own life and, although he was obviously fond of his father, he didn't have a close connection to him the way that her own boys had had with their dad.

The difference was even more marked when she met Cameron's girls. They came together, Rosie and Stella, with their boyfriends, requesting a meeting at a café so that, Noelle thought, they could make a quick escape rather than having to linger over a meal. The girls were polite and curious, talked about themselves and asked her questions about New Zealand, but they didn't ask a single thing about how Cameron and Noelle had met, or about their current relationship. She was relieved that they weren't hostile, and they kissed their father on the cheek when they eventually left, but it made her sad when she thought about her own girls, and how close they'd been to Hugh. She'd thought that her and Hugh's relationship with their children was very normal, but she could see now that it had been unusual in its closeness, and still was, with all of them living in the same town, seeing her almost every day. She should count her blessings for that more, she told herself. She took her happiness far too much for granted.

Cameron had been on edge while the girls were there, and he seemed relieved when they left. He hadn't spoken to Noelle about them, but she wondered whether he'd been worried that they might be accusatory and defensive of their mother. What a shame that the two girls didn't appreciate their father more. No doubt they blamed him for not being present when they were young, and they obviously had a point. But she couldn't see the sense in carrying that resentment through adulthood, because your parents never live forever, and she knew one day they would regret not spending time with him.

The next day, two days from the end of her holiday, he finally took her to Subaqueous, which occupied a whole floor on a tall office building in Lower Thames Street, overlooking the river, not far from the Tower of London in one direction and London Bridge in the other. She could see as soon as he walked in the respect that his employees held for him, and everyone was ready with a smile or a wave to welcome them. He introduced her to everyone and took her through to his office, which had a splendid view across the city.

More than his apartment, this place held his presence, and she immediately knew that when he was in the city he spent most of his time there. Shelves heaved with well-thumbed books about all aspects of archaeology, and the walls contained large photographs of various wrecks in the process of being lifted. Although the office was modern, all chrome and glass, his desk was oak and looked like an antique, and it was filled with papers and files. She was pleased to see a frame in the corner with photos of each of his children. All around were mementoes of his travels; rugs and pots and tiny statues from all over the world, including a large glass cabinet showcasing replicas of ancient coins. There were also several drawings of wrecks, and she remembered then that he'd liked to sketch, and he obviously passed some time while he was travelling drawing the sites he was working on.

"What do you think?" He'd sat at his desk and was opening some letters, smiling as she wandered around.

"It's very you." She flashed him a smile as she noticed that he'd put the model of Gandalf that he'd bought in Wellington on his desk. "More so than your apartment."

"I spend a lot more time here."

"I guessed that. You could move a bed in here and save a lot of money on your flat."

He laughed. "That's true. You don't like the flat?"

"It's lovely. It's just not very… homely."

"I'm not a homely kind of guy," he said wryly, turning to open a cabinet of files.

She pondered on the words as she picked up a replica of a small Roman oil lamp and turned it over in her hands. Would he have said those words if she'd never left? Would they have built a home together, had children, had a happy family life? Or would they have drifted apart the same way he had with his ex, the flame dying until there was barely a spark to be seen?

"Good morning."

She turned at the sound of a female voice to see a woman standing in the doorway. She was average height, slender, dressed in an expensive gray suit that immediately made Noelle feel scruffy in her jeans and hoodie. She had short platinum-blonde hair in a stylish cut, immaculate makeup, and a look that was not openly hostile but was not particularly friendly either. She looked so like Rosie and Stella that Noelle knew instantly who it was. *Talk of the devil…*

"Lara." Cameron got hurriedly to his feet and rounded the table, although he didn't walk over to her. "What are you doing here?"

"I came to say hello." Her cool gaze passed over them both before settling on Noelle. "The girls said they'd met you yesterday and that you were only here for a few more days, and I thought I couldn't let you go without meeting you."

Cameron cleared his throat. "Noelle, this is Lara, my ex-wife. Lara, this is Noelle Goldsmith."

"Very formal," Lara said. "I think we've guessed who the other is." She held out a hand, and Noelle shook it. "Are you enjoying your stay?"

"It's been fun," Noelle said, hoping she looked as cool as the other woman, even though her heart was leaping about in her chest. "Apart from the weather."

"Yes, it's been a wet November. They're saying it might be a white Christmas this year."

"Wow. I haven't seen a white Christmas in… a long time." Next to her, Noelle felt Cameron stiffen—the last Christmas they'd spent together it had snowed. But he didn't say anything.

"Excuse me." A young man put his head around the door. "Mr. Taylor, would you have a moment for Mr. Brooks? He's popped in and he wants someone to take a look at the contract."

"Not now," Cameron said irritably, glancing nervously at the two women in his office.

But Noelle gave him a smile. "Go on. I'm sure we'll be fine for a couple of minutes."

The young man cleared his throat. "Mr. Brooks has already rung several times, and he's rather insistent…"

Cameron hesitated, his eyes meeting hers as if he didn't believe her. Then he turned on his heel and left the room.

Lara watched him go, then took a few steps into the room. "Shall we sit?" she asked.

"Sure." Noelle led the way to the other end of the office, and perched on the edge of one of the chairs. Lara did the same. Noelle's mouth had gone dry. What did the other woman want?

They studied each other for a moment. Cameron had been married to this woman, Noelle thought. He'd pledged to love her for the rest of his life, had given her three children. It made her feel funny inside to think of him being so close to someone else. For the first time she understood how he must feel about her being with Hugh.

Finally Lara smiled. "It's good to meet you at last. I've often wondered if you've changed much over the years, and I can see now that you haven't."

Changed? Noelle frowned, puzzled. She was sure she'd never met Lara before.

"I sometimes wonder if my life would have been different if Cameron hadn't been my first love," Lara said. "I knew he'd had other lovers, of course—he was thirty when I met him. But in my naïvety I assumed he hadn't loved any of them, otherwise why wasn't he still with them? If he'd told me about you right at the beginning, I might have had some warning, but I didn't find out about you until it was too late."

There was no bitterness in her voice, just a kind of tired acceptance. Was she saying that his feelings for Noelle were the reason their marriage hadn't worked? Noelle's face warmed.

"You have three lovely children," she said, trying to move the conversation onto something easier. "Josh is so like Cameron, and your girls are very like you, both very beautiful."

Lara's lips curved up. She studied Noelle curiously, her eyes wistful. "Rosie said he could hardly take his eyes off you."

Noelle opened and shut her mouth again.

"It's all right," Lara said softly. "I'm not here to make trouble. Cameron and I are in the past now. I'm pleased that he's found you again. He's been unhappy for so long. What are you going to do? Are you moving to London?"

Noelle shook her head slowly. "I have five kids in New Zealand, and a grandchild. And several on the way. My life is there."

"What will you do?"

"I… don't know. I expect we'll keep in touch."

"Poor Cameron," Lara whispered. "He'll be heartbroken. He ruined his marriage for you. And now he's going to lose you again."

Noelle felt the first twinges of resentment. "That's not fair. We parted over thirty years ago. I'm not going to take the blame for everything that's happened in his life since then."

"That's fair enough. Does he know you're going to leave?"

"I told him when I came here that I wouldn't be staying."

"You know Cameron—he'll be thinking he can talk you around. He won't be expecting you to up and leave."

Noelle got to her feet, her stomach churning. "I think you should leave."

Lara stood and picked up her purse. "I'm just saying it like it is. I still care for him, and I want him to be happy. He's pined for you his whole life. I can only imagine what went through his head when he saw you. Let him down lightly, okay?"

Noelle said nothing. Lara nodded, turned, and walked out.

Shaking a little, Noelle sank back onto the chair. She took a breath and blew it out. *He'll be thinking he can talk you around.* She'd known that was the case, of course, deep down. Everything he'd said about having a long-distance relationship, of flying out to meet each other a couple of times a year, it had all been a way to talk her into coming with him while he planned how to convince her to stay. That's what the two weeks had been—a chance for him to show her how wonderful it could be.

She looked up to see him standing there watching her, leaning against the doorway. He came in and walked over to her, his hands in his pockets.

"She's gone," Noelle said.

"I saw her leave. I'm so sorry I left you with her. She's upset you."

"No. She was fine. It wasn't that."

"What did she say?"

"She said 'I've often wondered if you've changed much over the years, and I can see now that you haven't.' What did she mean by that? I've never met her before."

He looked away, out of the window, to where the dark-gray Thames swept beneath London Bridge. He was silent for a long time. Then, finally, he walked over to his desk. He bent and opened the bottom drawer and took out a folder. After extracting a folded piece of A3 paper, he brought it over to her.

Noelle opened it. It was a sketch of her, done by Cameron in his room at the university. She'd been lying on the bed, curled up in the covers, and he'd sat by the window and sketched her in about thirty minutes. It was a good likeness, and captured the way her hair had been at the time, falling around her face, her lips curved in a smile as she watched him draw.

"She found it," he said. "About a year after we were married."

"Oh."

"She asked who it was. I told her about you. She gave it back to me and said, 'I see,' and she never mentioned it until I came home after she'd told me she was having an affair. She asked me then how she was supposed to live in a marriage where my heart was taken by someone else, and I knew who she meant. I said she was wrong, but she wasn't. It's always been you, Noelle."

He spoke simply, without any drama. She looked at the drawing, her throat tightening as she thought of how happy she'd been back then, how naïve.

"Why did you keep it?" she whispered.

He didn't reply. He took it from her, replaced it in the folder, and put it back in his desk. Then he switched off the light, took her hand, and led her out.

"Let's have dinner at the apartment tonight," he said. "We'll get takeout, Thai, maybe? And watch a movie. What do you think?"

She nodded and let him lead her out of the building, into the cold November afternoon. When she'd first arrived, she'd been overwhelmed by London, by its bright lights and busy-ness, by its glamor. Now, though, as they walked to the nearest Tube station, she thought how dark the city was compared to her home. There was more sky in New Zealand, it seemed. It felt as if the sun shone there all the time. London was dark, dingy, and dirty, and it covered its loneliness in a layer of glitz, like a woman with bad skin who smeared her foundation an inch thick.

Suddenly she felt immensely homesick, missing her quiet house, her garden with its veggie patches, the Bay of Islands Brides shop with its sparkling lights and beautiful gowns, the friendly people and her wonderful family, who must be missing her too, even though they professed they weren't.

Could she live here? She boarded the underground train with Cameron and held onto the rail as people packed themselves in like matches in a box. Nobody smiled, nobody looked at their neighbor. The train doors whooshed shut and it rattled off, thundering along in the darkness, people getting on and off, so many people playing out the dramas of their lives.

Cameron puts his arm around her shoulder and turned her to face him, and she knew he was reading her mood, and wanted to comfort her. She rested her cheek on his chest, feeling his lips on her hair, and closed her eyes. London wasn't her home anymore. But her heart still belonged to Cameron. It always had, and it always would.

What was she going to do?

Chapter Twenty-Three

Cameron knew that Lara had upset Noelle, albeit possibly unwittingly, and he worried that it was going to spoil their evening. Sure enough, she was quiet all the way back to the apartment, but once they'd ordered the Thai takeout, poured themselves a glass of wine each, and chosen a movie, she brightened a bit and was soon talking to him about the films she'd seen recently.

They ate their meal and drank their wine, and Cameron felt his thoughts and emotions settle like silt that had been stirred up at the bottom of a river.

Lara had been unable to resist taking a peek at the woman whom she knew he'd always loved, and it had been a shock for Noelle to see his ex, that was all. In an odd way, he was glad they'd met. It felt like the closing of a door, the end of one phase in his life, and the beginning of another.

Noelle curled up beside him, resting her head on his shoulder, and he thought how he would feel if he discovered that this was it, this was how he was going to spend the rest of his life. He wouldn't want to leave her when he had to travel. Would she come with him? Spend her days shopping or looking around the various cities while he worked?

He shifted on the sofa, feeling a twinge of guilt at the thought of her bridal shop that she'd worked so hard to set up. It was just a management role though, wasn't it? It wasn't as if she made the dresses. Anyone could run the shop. And her children weren't teens anymore. Her boys were grown and had busy jobs. No doubt her girls would miss her. But kids had to learn to stand on their own two feet at some point. Few people were lucky enough to have their mother living around the corner, ready to come running whenever they had a problem.

She couldn't just go back to her old life. It was crazy to think that was even a possibility now they'd found each other again. Guilt would play a factor, of course; she'd feel uneasy at the thought of leaving her grandchildren, especially with more grandchildren on the way. But they could fly back, couldn't they? Money was no issue, and it was only twenty-four hours to get across the world now. Distance meant nothing anymore.

His fingers tightened on her shoulder, and he placed a kiss on her hair. He wasn't going to let her go. He absolutely refused to.

She nestled against him, her breasts pressing against his chest, and he felt the familiar stirring as the lusty tiger inside him reared his head and yawned. He'd thought that maybe after they'd slept together a few times this hunger would have abated, but it showed no signs of doing so thus far.

The movie hadn't quite finished, but Cameron had had enough. He slid a finger beneath Noelle's chin and lifted it so she was looking into his eyes, and then he kissed her.

What was it about this woman that made him feel so possessive? He still felt like a twenty-year-old, ready to call out any man who dared look in her direction, intent on winning his woman. He slid his hand into her hair and held her there while he claimed her mouth, delving his tongue inside, needing to own her, to show her that she was his.

"Mmm..." she murmured, "slowly or you'll singe my eyebrows," but he was in no mood to play it safe tonight.

Standing, he turned off the movie, ignoring her protests that it hadn't ended, and pulled her to her feet. He led her through to the bedroom, leaving the lights off and filling the room with the light from the waxing moon.

"Cameron..." she whispered.

He took the hem of her T-shirt and lifted it up her body and over her hair, then dropped it to the ground. Next he removed her jeans, leaving her standing there in a pretty set of coral-colored underwear. He unclipped her bra and slid off her panties until she stood before him naked. Then he said, "Climb on the bed."

He took off his T-shirt as she did so, then removed his jeans. He opened the bedside drawer, stared at something he'd put in there earlier, then pushed it to one side and took out something else—one of his ties.

Noelle's eyebrows rose.

"Lay back," he said softly.

Her teeth tugged at her bottom lip.

He climbed onto the bed and leaned over her. "Are you going to do as you're told?"

Her eyes met his, challenging, questioning, with a flare of excitement that always set him alight. She gave a little shake of her head.

Laughing, Cameron took her left wrist and tied the tie around it neatly, slotted the other end through one of the bars of the headboard, then pulled it, raising her hand and forcing her to lie back. She fought him, sort of, trying to roll away, but he easily managed to loop the other end around her left wrist, and then he sat back with triumph, watching her face flush as he raked her with his gaze.

"I'm going to leave you like this," he said, leaning forward to kiss her lips before beginning to kiss down her body. "Tied to my bed for the rest of our days. Ready for me to use whenever I want."

She gave a soft moan as he closed his mouth over a nipple and sucked.

"Slowly," he scolded, swapping to the other one. "I'm going to play with you tonight, until you can't stand any more. Until you beg me to take you." Fierce, triumphant lust surged through him, and he teased her nipples until she squirmed, then continued to kiss down her body, taking his time to brush his lips and tongue over every inch of her skin.

By the time he reached her hips she was breathing heavily, but he moved to the end of the bed and started on her toes, and she gave a sigh of longing.

"Not yet," he murmured, and he proceeded to kiss each toe in turn before trailing his tongue up the arch of her foot, around her ankle bone, and up her calf. He did the same with her other foot, gradually leading up her thighs, only then allowing himself the reward of lowering between her legs.

"Is this what you want?" he asked, bending his head and placing soft kisses over her mound.

"Yes," she whispered.

"Tell me this is what you want."

She sighed. "This is what I want."

He lowered his head, touched his lips to her silky skin, then slid his tongue into her folds.

She cried out and arched her back, and he lifted his head, running his fingers over the soft skin of her thigh.

"Slowly," he said.

She opened her eyes and stared at the ceiling, and he chuckled. Carefully, deliberately, he ran his tongue lightly up to her clit and circled it, then lifted his head again and watched her.

Time and again he did it, arousing her to the edge, then stopping to kiss her thigh until she relaxed back into the bedclothes.

He was hard as rock and desperate to plunge into her, but he felt this fierce need to show her that he had this power. The thought of being able to dole it out, to have her know that he was in control of her pleasure, made him smile with smug satisfaction.

"Tell me what you want," he said silkily, when he saw her flex her hands and tug at the ties.

"Please…" She twisted on the bed.

"Tell me you're mine," he said, and blew warm breath over her clit, making her shudder. "Tell me you'll always be mine."

"I'm yours," she whispered, her breaths coming hard and fast.

Cameron pushed up, reached for a condom, and rolled it on, conscious of her big green eyes watching him. "Turn over," he said.

"How?" she said, gesturing at her tied hands.

In answer he lifted her and turned her onto her front, then moved between her legs.

He pressed the tip of his erection into her folds, then lowered down, sliding his arms beneath her. Kissing her neck, he touched his tongue to her skin, over her pulse, and then sucked at the spot. She cried out, trying to push against him.

Slowly, he slid into her, a fraction at a time, making them both sigh and groan until he was fully sheathed. "Oh yeah," he said, "Jesus, you feel good. Oh, Noelle." He pulled back until he was almost out of her, then thrust forward again. "This is what it's all about. I think about this night and day. I think I will keep you tied to my bed." He plunged into her, feverish with passion, dizzy with desire, hungry and desperate and fierce. "Tell me you love me."

She groaned and buried her face in the pillow.

"Tell me," he said harshly.

"I love you," she said. "I love you. Cameron, please…"

Thrilled, victorious, he thrust hard, driving them both to a glorious climax. She clenched hard around him and cried out, and he held her chin and thrust his tongue into her mouth as his body tightened and pulsed, wanted to consume her, to make her his, to make sure she never, ever left his side again.

There was a second of ultimate sweetness, a peak of pleasure, and then the moment passed, leaving him panting, sweating, heavy on top of her. She lay limp on the pillow, but he didn't move, loving the feel of her spent beneath him, the two of them fucked in more ways than one.

He lay there for a long while. Then, finally, he turned his head and looked at the bedside table. Carefully, he withdrew from her and disposed of the condom, then he reached over and took out the box.

He brought it back, curving his body around her, his chest to her back, and put it on the pillow.

Noelle opened her eyes and looked at it.

"Open it," he whispered.

She flexed her tied hands.

He reached out and flipped the lid open for her. The ring glinted in the moonlight. The eight-carat diamond was surrounded by a halo of smaller diamonds on a platinum band. It had cost him over one hundred thousand pounds. He'd have paid ten times that to get what he wanted.

"Marry me," he said.

She lifted onto her elbows as best she could. "Untie me."

He kissed her shoulder. "Not until you say yes."

She shifted on the bed, turning a little so she could look up at him. They stared at each other for a long, long while.

"You're serious," she said eventually.

"Of course I'm serious."

"You really want to marry me?"

"I've wanted to marry you for thirty-three years." He kissed her nose. "I love you. You're all I want in the world."

"If I move to London."

He tipped his head to the side. "Would that be so bad? It's not 1985 anymore. I fly around the world all the time. We'd spend some time in New Zealand, obviously. But I can't move there, sweetheart. It'll be much easier for you to live here."

"Easier for you," she said.

He pursed his lips. This conversation wasn't going as well as he'd planned. He'd thought the ring would dazzle her, even if only a little. He'd thought the proposal would win her heart.

"I have a life too," she said. "A family who needs me. A business to run."

He felt the first flicker of impatience. "Anyone can run the bridal shop, Noelle. You've left your friend in charge, haven't you?"

"That's not the point."

He pushed up. "Maybe not. The point is whether you're really going to walk away from me. We've waited all these years for this. Are you really telling me it's over?"

She opened her mouth to reply, and at that moment her iPad began ringing, announcing a call on FaceTime. He glanced over and saw it was Roberta, her eldest daughter.

"Untie me," Noelle said.

"Not until you agree to marry me," he replied as calmly as possible.

She flexed her hands in the tie. "Cam, come on. I need to speak to Roberta."

"Right now, we are more important than anything else in your life," he told her fiercely.

Her eyes went cold, and he immediately knew he'd said the wrong thing.

"Cameron Taylor," she snapped, "I'm fucking serious. Untie my fucking hands."

With some shock, he realized she wasn't playing. Immediately, he undid the ties, and she sat up and rolled over, rubbing her wrists. She picked up the iPad, which had stopped ringing. Then she got up, walked into the bathroom, and closed the door.

Cameron pulled on his underwear and track pants and walked over to the window. He'd played it all wrong. He'd thought she'd respond to a declaration of passion and love, that he'd win her over with the force of his personality. That she wouldn't be able to turn him down.

Despair swept over him. What a fucking idiot.

Chapter Twenty-Four

Noelle pulled on the bathrobe hanging on the back of the door and sank onto the toilet seat. Her hands shook, and her throat was constricted with anger and frustration.

She thought of the ring he'd produced and put her face in her hands. It must have cost him an absolute fortune. A beautiful bauble, meant to dazzle her into accepting his proposal. He wanted her. She was in no doubt of that. He would do anything to keep her, and that included manipulating her in any way he could think of to force her to stay.

She swallowed hard, determined not to cry, took a deep breath, and blew it out slowly. She had to think very carefully about this.

Cameron was the CEO of a huge business that he'd devoted his life to. He wasn't able to drop everything to run to the other side of the world. She couldn't blame him for that. She was just insulted at his insistence that anyone could run her shop. Technically, he was right. But that didn't take account of the fact that it was her business, her vision. Hers and the girls. She'd spent years building it up to what it was now, and she knew it was only going to continue to grow. She was proud of her achievement, and she didn't want to walk away from it.

Right now, we are more important than anything else in your life. That angered her, too. It was an arrogant thing to say, even though she understood why he'd said it. But it didn't matter that they'd known each other years ago; she'd been with him three weeks. Her family was her world. She knew she wasn't indispensable—they were all grown up and would cope if she no longer lived around the corner. But she liked being a part of their lives. Being there to babysit, to help out. She liked being needed.

Cameron was arrogant, overconfident, and selfish, and he thought he could talk her into doing what he wanted. He'd always put his own needs first.

But despite that, she still loved him. She wanted to be with him. But she couldn't think how to make it work.

A stubborn piece of her didn't want to accept his proposal because she didn't want him to win. She didn't want to admit that her life was less important than his. And yet was that really a hill to die on? One of them had to give way, and it wasn't going to be him.

So what it came down to was: how much did she want him?

She looked at the iPad, swiped the screen, and returned the missed call.

Roberta answered within a few rings. "Mum! I'm so sorry, did I wake you?"

"No, no. We haven't gone to bed yet." Noelle's throat tightened again at the sight of her eldest daughter, curled up on the sofa with a cat on her lap. "Where's Angus?"

"He's gone to work. I'm off in a minute. I wanted a chat first." She smiled, but Noelle thought it seemed brittle.

"What's up?"

"Not much. How's life in the UK?"

"Busy. Cameron took me to Subaqueous today." She told her a little about the office. "And we had Thai takeout tonight."

"Oh, lovely. I haven't had Thai for ages. So… one more night, eh?"

Noelle nodded slowly. Her return flight was booked for Wednesday.

"Not tempted to stay?" Roberta asked brightly. But Noelle saw the hint of worry in her eyes.

"What's happened?" she asked softly.

"Nothing! Nothing at all. Not much, anyway." Roberta glanced away, out at her garden, her shoulders slumping. "Everyone keeps saying we shouldn't bother you. But we know each other well enough by now, don't we? You'd rather know what's going on, wouldn't you?"

"Always, sweetheart. Tell me."

"Most of it's stupid stuff. It's so odd not having you here. I mean, it's nothing that we can't handle, but normally I'd talk to you about it, and you always seem to know what to do." She ran a hand through her hair. "I think there's something in the air, that's all. Everyone seems on edge. Elliot's been acting weird. Bianca and Freddie had a big argument. They're okay, but the air's a bit frosty."

"What about?"

"Oh, he wants to get married. She thinks they should wait. Something like that. She's not said much, but you know something's wrong when she goes quiet."

Noelle frowned. "And you, are you okay?"

Roberta gave a small shrug. "I had a phone call from Ian yesterday."

Ian was the older married ex who, unbeknown to Noelle and Hugh, had kept Roberta as a mistress for many years in Auckland. He'd tried to get her to start seeing him again a few months ago, declaring that he'd left his wife, but luckily Angus had been there to step in and show Roberta what true love looked like. Noelle had been relieved. She'd been close to driving down to Auckland with an axe and a black bag to sort Ian out herself.

Now she went cold at the thought that he'd been in contact with her daughter again. "Does Angus know?"

"God, no. He'd be furious."

"What did Ian want?"

"The usual. Begging me to go back to him."

"Are you…" Noelle's mouth went dry. "Are you thinking about it?"

Roberta's expression softened. "No, Mum. Don't worry. I don't feel anything for him anymore, and I have Angus now. I love Angus with all my heart. It's upsetting, that's all, having to deal with it. I just wish he'd leave me alone."

"You should call the police," Noelle said, knowing even as she said it that Roberta would never consider it. Her daughter might not love Ian anymore, but she had not that long ago, and once you loved someone, you always felt something for them. Noelle knew that.

"Is that it?" she said. "Everyone else okay? Dominic?"

"He's fine. Overworked I think, according to Fliss, but fine."

"And Phoebe?" At Roberta's hesitation, she knew she'd finally ferreted out the truth. "What's happened to Phoebe?"

"She's had a little bleeding," Roberta said softly. "She's okay, the baby's still fine. Angus has told her to rest, so she's staying home for a few days. She's a bit panicky, that's all. But she didn't want me to tell you. She doesn't want you to worry. And maybe I shouldn't have, after all there's nothing you can do from over there. I just thought you should know."

Noelle stood and looked at her reflection in the bathroom mirror, seeing her pale face, the concern in her eyes. Phoebe was about fourteen weeks pregnant, so technically out of the three-month danger zone, but of course pregnancy was dangerous no matter how many weeks along a woman was. And she'd had trouble conceiving because of her accident, so of course she was going to be super worried that she would lose it.

"I'm sorry," Roberta said. "Did I do the right thing?"

"Of course." Noelle spoke briskly. "As you say, there's not much I can do from here. But I'll be home on Thursday. Try and encourage her to rest until I get there. Then we can decide whether we think she needs to see someone."

"All right." Roberta's face showed her relief, and Noelle melted a little inside. Her sons and daughters were grown and could cope on their own, but that didn't mean that the presence of their mother wasn't comforting. She wanted to be there to help them. It wasn't that she didn't love Cameron enough. It was that, as she'd grown older, duty and responsibility had become more important than anything else. Cameron had been wrong there. The most important thing in her life was her children, and if he couldn't understand that, he didn't know her at all.

She said goodbye to Roberta, promising to phone her again before she left, and turned off her iPad. She splashed some water on her face and blew her nose. Then she went out into the bedroom.

Cameron sat in a chair by the window, sipping from a tumbler of whisky. He turned as she came out though, placed the glass on the table by his side, and stood. "Everything okay?"

"No big disasters. Phoebe's had a little bleeding apparently." She'd told him all about Phoebe's accident, and that she was pregnant. "She's okay, just needs some rest."

"Good." He nodded with satisfaction, and right then she knew that he had no idea what she was feeling.

"I can't do it, Cam." She shoved her hands into the pockets of the robe and hunched her shoulders. Her gaze slid over to the bed. The ring still rested in its box on the pillow, next to the tie he'd tried to use to convince her to stay. "I can't marry you, and I can't stay. I'm very sorry."

He stared at her for a moment. Then he bent and picked up the whisky, finished off the glass, and walked out of the bedroom.

She followed him into the kitchen, where he'd retrieved the bottle from the cupboard and was busy pouring himself another glass. He held the bottle up to her, and she shook her head.

"So that's it?" He pushed the bottle away and leaned against the counter. "I don't get a say in it?"

"What do you want to say?"

He frowned and glared at her. "Don't you think we should discuss it? Talk about it?"

"You mean I should listen while you try to convince me to stay?"

"That's not fair."

"Isn't it?" Indignation flared inside her. "Cameron, you've not made any commitment toward me."

His eyes widened. "Do you have any idea how much that ring cost?"

"I'm flattered that you would think to spend so much money on me. And I'm not saying I'm not grateful for everything you've spent on me over the last few weeks. I've had the time of my life, and it's been great. But I'm not talking about money. You don't show someone how much you love them by how much you spend on them." At his confused look, she continued, "Not once have you talked about coming with me to New Zealand. Not once."

He stared at her. "I can't. I have a business to run."

"So have I."

"It's hardly the same."

"Because yours is so important and mine is a silly little bridal shop?" He didn't reply, and she knew that was what he was thinking. "That's insulting on so many levels. It doesn't matter if I was working as a waitress or cleaning offices if that job was important to me."

Impatience flickered on his face. "That's fair enough, but if we want to be together, we have to compromise, don't we? You said that yourself."

"Where's your compromise, Cam? I'd be giving up my business, my family... What would you be giving up?"

He hesitated, then looked away.

"Last time," she said softly, "all those years ago when I said my parents were moving to New Zealand... You never suggested coming with me then, either."

Now he looked exasperated. "I was halfway through a university course. My whole life was here."

"I know. And I know it would have been a difficult decision. But my point is that you never even mentioned it. And at the time, that was a major factor in my decision to leave."

He stared at her. "Are you saying that if I'd have offered to go with you, you might have stayed?" His bafflement was evident.

"I don't know. It would have meant a lot to me, I do know that. And because you didn't, I had to think about what I would be giving up not to see my parents. I loved you with all my heart. But you had stars in your eyes. You were going to do something amazing, I knew it. And I thought that if you weren't prepared to make that sacrifice for me, maybe, just maybe, what we had wasn't worth fighting for."

His jaw had dropped. Now he closed it firmly, his brows drawing together. "I can't believe you'd say that now. I was twenty, for fuck's sake! New Zealand felt like the end of the world—it still does! It's miles from anywhere, and my whole life was here."

She turned away, walked over to the cupboard, and began taking out her clothes. "I don't want to argue with you."

"What are you doing?"

"I'm going to go."

"Oh Jesus, don't be stupid."

She paused, then let her robe fall and started dressing.

"No, come on. Noelle." He walked over to her and took her top from her hand. "I'm not letting you go like this."

"It's not up to you," she snapped, snatching it back. "Are you really going to tie me to the bed to make me stay?"

"No, of course not. And I'm sorry that went awry. It was supposed to be fun, sexy... I was trying to show you how much I wanted you."

"You were trying to control me. I'm not eighteen anymore. I'm a grown woman, a mother, a grandmother. I have my own life now. And I don't want to live in London."

"You said you loved me," he pointed out.

She gave a humorless laugh as she tugged the top on. "A confession given under duress isn't worth anything."

"I was hardly torturing you!"

"Weren't you? You were practicing orgasm denial, Cameron. I'd have said anything at that point."

"So you don't love me?"

She opened her case, then paused and looked up at him. His eyes were full of pain and regret. She looked down and swallowed. "I do. You know I do. And it's been a great few weeks. I'm so glad you saw me at the ball. I don't regret our time spent together. But it's over." She started putting things into her case.

"Maybe I went too far," he said. "With the proposal. You weren't ready. I get that. I'm sorry. But can't we talk about our original plan? To keep in touch? See each other a few times a year?"

She was struggling to stay in control now, tears pricking her eyes, her throat hurting with emotion. "I can't. I'm sorry but I can't. It's too hard. I know that every time we were to part, you would try to convince me to stay."

"I won't, I swear."

"You would, and you know it. It's not going to work. It wasn't back then, and it won't now." She threw all the rest of her things in the case.

"Don't go. Please." He caught her arm. "You've still got one more night. Stay with me. Don't let's end it like this."

She stopped and turned to him, knotted up with anguish, but calm in her resolution. "I can't, Cam. You know I can't."

He looked into her eyes. Then he pulled her into his arms and buried his face in her hair.

Noelle hugged him for the last time. She pressed her cheek to his chest, listened to his heart, and closed her eyes. She wanted him, and she loved him as much as she had thirty-three years ago. But love shouldn't be this hard. She didn't want the drama and the conflicting emotions. She didn't want to have to be torn every time she was going to see him because she knew she'd have to leave him. It had all happened too late, and she was too old to deal with it now. She'd been foolish to think age didn't matter.

"Where will you go?" he asked.

"To Annie's." Her old school friend would be thrilled to put her up for the night.

She pushed back, and he let his hands drop. Turning, she hefted the case onto the floor and picked up her coat and purse. She walked about, making sure she had everything, averting her eyes from the ring on the pillow. Then she returned to get her case and wheeled it to the door. There she stopped and turned to look at him. He stood in the center of the room, lost and forlorn, his face filled with pain.

"I'm sorry," she said. "I had a lovely time, and thank you for taking me to all those wonderful places. I'll miss you."

She opened the door, went outside, and let it close behind her.

Chapter Twenty-Five

Ten days later

The San Jose galleon off the coast of Colombia was on the verge of being lifted.

Cameron was doing a final dive himself to survey the area. He'd already donned his wetsuit and breathing apparatus when he heard his phone ringing in the jacket pocket in the cabin of the boat.

The rest of the dive team weren't quite ready, so he took out the phone, saw it was Marcus, and answered it. "Hi."

"Hey. How's it going?"

"Just about to go down," Cameron said. "Last reccy. We'll definitely be starting next week."

"That's great news. A month ahead of schedule! They're gonna love us."

"One can only hope."

"How are you feeling?"

"Better." Cameron coughed. Almost as soon as Noelle had left he'd gotten a cold that had gone onto his chest, leaving him congested and stuffy.

"Are you sure you're ready to dive?"

"Stop fussing. You're not my mother." Cameron looked over the side. The cerulean sea lapped at the boat, glistening in the early morning sun. Usually he looked forward to these early dives and couldn't wait to get into the water. He'd never felt as if this was a job, and had never understood those people who dreaded going to work. But today he felt dull and restless. There was no flutter of excitement in his stomach at what he might find amidst the bare bones of the wreck, no joy at the thought of discovering the glint of gold.

"Well?" Marcus prompted. "Did you call?"

Cameron resisted the urge to throw the phone in the water. His friend was concerned and was trying to help, that was all. "No."

"Cam…"

"I'm not talking about this."

"Jesus. I'm going to have to put up with you being like a bear with a sore head for the rest of eternity, aren't I?"

"If you don't like being around me, there's an answer to that," Cameron snapped.

Marcus said nothing for a moment. Cameron closed his eyes.

"I'd better go," Marcus said eventually. "Lots to do."

"Yeah. Have a great day." Cameron switched off his phone and tossed it on top of his clothes in the cabin.

He strode out, his heart black and his mood low. Noelle had walked away from him a second time. What was the saying? Fool me once, shame on you. Fool me twice, shame on me? He was an idiot for thinking he could talk her into staying with him. She didn't love him—not enough, anyway. And despite Marcus's urgings, it was pointless to call her or try to stay in touch. She'd made her feelings clear, and he had to learn to accept his situation.

He didn't want to talk about Noelle, he didn't even want to think about her. And the best way to achieve that state of numbness—apart from whisky, which wasn't advisable when it was early morning and he was about to dive—was to get to work.

Within ten minutes he was in the water, heading down with his team toward the ship that lay with its back broken on the sandy seabed like a dead animal.

It wasn't a deep dive, maybe fifty feet or so, and he was down for about thirty minutes before he felt the first niggling sense of a problem.

Cameron had brushed away Marcus's query on whether he was ready to dive but, as his breathing became labored, he knew he hadn't fully recovered from the chest infection. He stopped working and waited for a moment. The visibility was poor around the wreck, and he couldn't see the other members of his team. He and his dive buddy, Ben, were normally not more than a few feet from each other, but he couldn't see him. There was an odd resistance to his breathing, no doubt from the chest infection.

And then, all of a sudden, there was no air at all.

In all his years of diving, Cameron had never had a problem with his air tanks. The last time he'd checked, about twenty-five minutes before, he'd had about 180 bars which should have been more than enough to see him through the dive. He turned in the water, searching for Ben, but swirls of silt clouded his vision. He tried a couple of strokes toward the surface, but his lungs were already burning, and he knew he wasn't going to make it.

Holy Jesus. He'd always thought himself a man in control of his emotions, but panic arced through him. He was going to die. He was going to drown here, at the bottom of the ocean across the other side of the world from the woman he loved. He'd put his pride first, and now he was paying the ultimate price. He would never see Noelle again, would never hold her in his arms or tell her he was sorry.

What a fucking tragedy.

*

Three days later

"Oh honey, how are you feeling?"

As soon as Cameron opened his front door, Rebecca walked up to him and put her arms around him. "We've been out of our minds with worry."

"What she said," Marcus told him, giving him a bear hug once his wife released him. "Dude, don't do that to me again."

"I'm not planning to," Cameron said wryly, gesturing for them to follow him in. "That was pretty scary."

"I can imagine." Rebecca sat on the sofa and Marcus sank beside her, putting the bottle of whisky they'd brought on the table. "Marcus said your dive buddy only made it with seconds to go."

Cameron sat opposite them and admired the bottle of expensive Ardbeg for a moment before turning his attention to them. He didn't want to return to the memory of that moment when he'd been convinced he'd die. He'd had nightmares every night since then, images of drowning and darkness, and it made him shudder whenever he thought about it.

But the two of them were his closest friends, and he wasn't going to tell them to go. "Yeah, that's right. I'd just got to the point where I was convinced I was done for, and then Ben appeared. He let me breathe from his octopus—that's a secondary demand valve on his own breathing apparatus," he told Rebecca, "and we slowly rose to the surface."

"What caused the problem?" she wanted to know.

"I had two tanks but the isolator valve on the manifold was closed, so I breathed the right tank until it was empty and then there was only the air left in my suit."

"You didn't do a shut-down drill before you went down?" Marcus asked.

"No." Cameron met his gaze and then dropped his own. He was ashamed to admit it. He hadn't waited for his chest infection to clear, and his mind hadn't been on the dive. For the first time ever, he'd not followed the correct procedure, and as a result he'd nearly died.

"How are you doing?" Marcus asked.

Cameron looked away, out of the window, conscious of the two of them exchanging glances.

"I'm sure it's normal to feel nervous about diving again," Rebecca said softly. "You need to get back on the horse, that's all."

"I don't know. I think I might be done." Cameron brought his gaze back to them.

Marcus studied him with a thoughtful expression. "Don't make a knee-jerk reaction. Bex is right; you'll be fine once you get in the water again."

"It's not that. I'm not scared of diving." It was a lie, although he'd never admit it to Marcus. He thought about the nightmares of being smothered by the cold, dark water and tried not to shudder. "But I'm fifty-four. I'm in relatively good health, or I was until I nearly drowned myself. We run a huge company with thousands of employees. I don't need to dive myself anymore. I think maybe it's time I took up a more managerial role."

"Of course it's up to you," Marcus said, glancing at his wife, who looked close to tears. "But your first love has always been the work—the real work, not the pen-pushing or the doing deals. You're the one who's always liked getting his hands dirty."

"I do. I did. But there are other ways I can get involved without physically going in the water. In fact that's what I wanted to talk to you about. I have an idea."

*

An hour later, Marcus and Rebecca had left, and although it was only seven p.m., Cameron was on his second glass of the Ardbeg.

He sat in the window overlooking the city of London, at the lights in the offices and homes. It would be Christmas in two weeks. He hadn't bought a tree or hung decorations since the kids were young. He missed the feeling he'd had as a child in the pit of his stomach when Christmas was approaching. The anticipation of the presents, the knowledge that Santa was checking his list, that Rudolph would soon be pulling the sleigh. He hated the fact that now he found Christmas carols annoying, and that the season felt so commercial it had lost its magic.

What would Christmas be like Down Under? Noelle had said that her family would be spending the day around the pool, having a barbecue. How weird was that? He couldn't imagine it being warm in December.

But the talk of a white Christmas in London had disappeared, and now the meteorologists were forecasting the usual cool, damp weather. He watched the rain patter on the window, and he thought that yes, maybe it would be nice to spend the festive season somewhere warm.

He picked up his phone and brought up the number he'd programmed in earlier that day. It had taken some searching online and a few phone calls, but he'd finally tracked it down.

He pressed the green button, and listened to it ring.

For a while, he didn't think anyone was going to answer it, but eventually a man said, "Hello?"

"Good morning." Cameron was surprised to discover he was nervous. "Is that Dominic Goldsmith?"

"Yes. Can I help you?"

"I hope so. My name is Cameron Taylor. I'm your mother's… friend."

"Oh! Wow. Hello. Are you calling from England?"

"Yes." He took a mouthful of whisky and let it burn down to his stomach, then stood and went over to the window. "I hope you don't mind me ringing you. It's not too early?"

"It's perfect timing—eight a.m. here. My wife and daughter have left for school and I was doing some paperwork before I left too. What can I do for you, Cameron?" Dominic sounded mellow and genial, with no hint of the suspicion or dislike Cameron had feared. He'd wondered whether the deacon would be judgmental, would resent how Cameron had treated his mother, but it didn't appear that way yet.

"I wondered if I could talk to you about Noelle."

"Sure." Dominic sounded amused. "Or you could call her direct. Do you have her number?"

"I do. And I would, but... I wanted to talk to you first. I know you're her eldest son, and that you're head of the family since your father passed."

"I don't know that my sisters would agree with that, but I know what you're saying."

"And... with your position..."

"You mean as deacon?"

"Yes... I was hoping for some... advice." He could almost picture the way Dominic's eyebrows were rising. It was not easy to ask a younger man for help. But after his accident, Cameron had discovered he was thinking about a lot of things very differently from the way he had before. Plus, the man was a counsellor as well as a deacon, so he figured Dominic might be able to help him in more ways than one.

"Of course," Dominic said.

"I know this sounds as if I'm fourteen, but I wondered whether Noelle had... you know... missed me at all. Has she spoken about me?"

To his relief, Dominic didn't laugh. Instead, he said softly, "Yes, of course. We had a long talk, the two of us, a few days after she arrived back."

"How is she?"

"She's broken-hearted."

Cameron blinked, surprised by the direct comment.

"You didn't think she would be?" Dominic asked at his silence.

"I wasn't sure. We didn't part well."

"She told me a little about it. She doesn't blame you, Cameron."

"But it's my fault," he said hoarsely, full of emotion.

"From what I understand, she's upset about the situation. She hoped there would be an easy solution, but the two of you have responsibilities and interests that you're unable to give up. She's very sad, that's all, disappointed that she found you but that it was impossible to make it work."

Cameron's legs suddenly felt weak, and he sat in the chair again. "It's not impossible."

Dominic paused. "What do you mean?"

"I've been doing a lot of thinking. Tell me, as a man of the church, do you believe in near-death experiences?"

"Well, there's obviously a precedent in the Bible for God bringing men back from the dead—the prophets Elijah and Elisha both raised boys back to life. Jesus raised Lazarus. And of course Jesus was resurrected himself. But I'm guessing you're not looking for a philosophical discussion. Has something happened?"

Cameron told him briefly about his experience on the dive. "I didn't see lights or anything. I'm not claiming I actually died. But… I feel differently about things now."

"That's common with events like this, when a person experiences severe trauma, or recovers from what they thought was a terminal illness, for example. It makes us reevaluate our lives. Things that we thought were important suddenly appear of little value when life itself is threatened."

"That's it exactly." Cameron felt a rush of relief that Dominic understood. "Until then, I assumed it was over with Noelle because she wasn't willing to give up her life for me, and I didn't even question whether I could give up mine for her. I run a huge company, and my whole life revolved around it."

"And now?"

He felt a lightness of spirit that he wasn't entirely sure wasn't due to speaking to the deacon, who seemed exceptionally wise for his relative youth. "And now, as you say, I'm reevaluating. I have an idea, and I'd like to ask your opinion, and maybe your help, too."

Chapter Twenty-Six

Noelle finished serving a mother and daughter who'd bought one of Bianca and Phoebe's dresses and smiled as they went off to the coffee shop to chat and giggle over their purchase while they had a drink.

She had the best job in the world, she thought. One of the happiest jobs, certainly. It didn't matter that a third of all marriages supposedly ended in divorce. Her shop was about the promise of a beautiful relationship that—at the point it began—both parties were convinced would last forever.

Her smile faded, and she turned, went into her office, sat in her chair, and picked up a financial report she'd been meaning to read.

After a few minutes, she put it down and stared out of the window.

It had been over two weeks since she'd left England. Sixteen days since she'd said goodbye to the man she loved. And she hadn't heard from him at all. Not once.

What had she expected? She'd told him it was over, and that there was no point in them staying in touch because it was too hard. Why should he call her? What would be the point in him badgering her to keep in touch when it was clear things wouldn't work out?

It all made sense, but it didn't stop it hurting. What was he doing? Was he off working, diving somewhere in the Mediterranean or the Atlantic or the Indian Ocean, finding himself a woman to hook up with in each city? She fought against a fierce stab of jealousy. Was he thinking of her at all?

These kinds of thoughts had gone around and around in her head since she'd returned. On the plane, as it had taken off, she'd found herself in tears, crying for what might have been, for her past, for her future, she wasn't sure. Over the twenty-six hours of her journey, though, she'd forced herself to come to terms with her situation, and had steeled herself to accept it. She'd made the choice. She couldn't now cry because she didn't like the outcome.

But sitting there, in her beautiful sunlit shop, hearing her daughters laughing next door in the café and feeling as if she should be the happiest woman in the world, all Noelle felt was incredibly sad.

Had she made the wrong decision? She picked up a pen and doodled on a notepad. There was no doubt that her family had been relieved to see her back.

Phoebe had cried when her mother had walked in, and although she'd recovered quickly and was now back working at the shop, Noelle knew her daughter felt better for having her there. She'd fussed around her a little, made her soup, tidied up her house, maybe released some of her tension, which was good for the baby, and Phoebe seemed better for it.

Noelle had sat down with Bianca and had a long talk, during which Bianca admitted she was concerned that Freddie was offering marriage as a knee-jerk because he'd found somewhere he felt comfortable that was so unlike his home with his parents. She was worried he might change his mind after a while and wish he'd played the field a bit more. Noelle told her honestly that she'd never seen a man with stars in his eyes as much as Freddie Brooks, and Bianca ought to grab him and hang onto him, because love like that didn't come around very often. The two of them had now set a date for the wedding the following year, and were happy as could be.

She'd had a long talk with Roberta and had finally convinced her to tell Ian that she was blocking his calls, and that she wouldn't reply to any emails or messages from him. Cutting herself loose would be good for her relationship with Angus, Noelle told her. She knew that Roberta didn't have any feelings for Ian anymore. She loved Angus, and the two of them were getting married in the New Year. But the past dug its claws into you, and sometimes it was hard to tear yourself free. Roberta had agreed and done as her mother suggested, and now she and Angus seemed blissfully happy.

Elliot was another matter. He'd been quiet, distant, and pretty much absent since her return apart from a brief visit after she landed. Noelle knew something was going on with him, but at the moment he wasn't in the mood to communicate, so she'd told him that she was always available if he needed to talk, and had left him alone to sort himself out.

Dominic and Emily were fine, and Fliss felt well with her pregnancy, so that was good.

So her children were either happy or sorting themselves out. But almost everything she'd done she could have said over the phone. Did she really need to be there?

She sat back in her chair and looked through the door at the shop. It was a beautiful summer's day, and the sequins on the dresses in the window sparkled. They had to rotate the displays almost daily because the sunlight was so strong and would damage the dresses, but Noelle didn't mind. She loved December in the Northland, with all the pohutukawa trees donning their festive red flowers, and the bay growing busier with tourists excited to be in paradise.

When she'd first moved to New Zealand, it had seemed bizarre to have Christmas in summer. She'd missed the turkey with all the trimmings, and the feeling of warming her toes on the fire as she watched all the old Christmas movies. Here they still played Christmas songs, but it was surreal singing 'chestnuts roasting on an open fire' when the weather was so warm she had to turn the aircon on at night.

But all her kids had grown up Kiwis, and to them it was perfectly normal to spray snow from a can on the windows while wearing T-shirts or bikinis. They'd still believed in Santa Claus, even if all the Kiwi children's books portrayed him in a vest and shorts and wearing gumboots, with a sleigh drawn by sheep.

And now she was used to it too, and she couldn't imagine spending Christmas in the UK, where it so rarely snowed, and was always wet, cool, and gray. In London they had approximately 1500 hours of sunshine a year; in Kerikeri she had over two thousand. She'd missed those extra hours when she'd been there with Cameron. The sky had seemed permanently gray. She'd missed the beautiful blue of the Northland.

She didn't want to go back. That was what it came down to. Her life was here. Her children. Her shop. And she was a Kiwi now, through and through. She loved her country, the weather, the people, who were so friendly and welcoming. She adored the relaxed way of life, the 'everything can wait while the sun's out' kind of attitude.

And yet, she loved Cameron too.

Jesus, what an awful decision to have to make. No wonder she was so knotted up.

Closing her eyes, she pictured him in her mind; his tall frame, his steel-gray hair, his gorgeous violet eyes. She remembered the way he kissed her, with just the right touch of forcefulness, telling her that he thought of her as his, and that he didn't want to let her go. He'd been no different in bed either, still passionate and insatiable, taking great delight in her body, despite her reticence about the way it had changed over the years.

God, she missed him so much. Was it possible that she really was being torn in two by this decision?

Not that there was a decision to make now. She'd made it, and even if she were to get back on the phone and beg him to have her back, she'd hurt his feelings—twice—and he might tell her to stick it where the sun didn't shine.

No, it was done. She had to learn to live with it, that was all.

Tears pricked her eyes. She sniffed hard, stood, and brushed down her skirt. She had work to do and it was a beautiful day. She wasn't going to sink into self-pity.

She went out into the shop as the door opened and the bell rang, and smiled to see her eldest son. "Dominic! Good morning. What are you doing here?"

"Just passing," he said. He came over and kissed her temple. "How are you?"

"Fine, fine. About to change the window display."

"I wondered if you had half an hour to spare? I could do with a chat?"

Her eyebrows rose. "Something wrong?"

"Mmm... not really. I could do with some advice."

"Okay." It was unusual for Dominic to come to her, but she was happy to help if she could. "Do you want to go into my office?"

"Actually I thought we could go out for a coffee, if that's okay?"

He didn't want the girls around while they talked. "Sure," she said, "Cathy won't mind covering for me." She collected her purse, popped her head into the café and asked her friend to keep an eye on the shop, and then followed Dominic out.

He'd parked down the road, and they got in the car, then headed through the town.

"I thought we'd go to the Partridge," he said.

Her heart sank a little as she remembered the last time she'd been there with Cameron, but she pushed the thought away. She'd have to get over those nostalgic memories and get on with her life. "That would be lovely. So... what's on your mind. Is Fliss feeling okay?"

"Oh, she's fine. It's nothing physical. I'm a bit worried about Emily, that's all."

"Emily?"

"Being jealous about the baby."

Noelle frowned. "I thought she was excited about having a little brother or sister?"

"She said she is, but deep down I'm not so sure."

"What has she said to worry you?"

He eased the car through the one-way section past the shops and headed out of town. "She goes quiet when we talk about the baby. I don't want her to feel as if we're pushing her out, but equally I don't want to hide anything from her."

"No, of course not. I have to admit, I'm still surprised by what you're saying. Emily's been over the moon every time I've seen her. She hasn't seemed concerned at all about the possibility of a sibling—quite the opposite. Lots of little girls like babies. They enjoy dressing them and feeding them. And anyway, Emily doesn't strike me as the jealous type. She's very sensible, and she loves Fliss so much."

Dominic navigated the roundabout and headed down the road toward the inlet. Palms and ferns lined the road, waving gently in the summer breeze. "You're probably right. I don't know why I'm so worried. I suppose it's something to do with it making her miss her mother more when she sees Fliss with the baby."

"I wouldn't worry about it until it happens," Noelle said as the car emerged at the basin and he headed it into the car park of the Partridge. "Because it probably won't. Worry is the darkroom where negatives develop, right?"

Dominic smiled as he parked and turned off the engine. "That's very true. You are a wise old woman."

"Hey, less of the old!" She laughed and got out of the car, joining her son as they headed toward the restaurant. "I might have a muffin. I'm feeling peckish."

"Mmm, me too."

They approached the wishing well, and she glanced up to see a man standing there. Oddly, he was facing them, watching them approach. She lifted her hand and shaded her eyes. And stopped.

Dominic bent and kissed her cheek. "Sorry for the subterfuge," he murmured.

Her heart racing, Noelle glanced at him with a wry smile. "Emily's fine, I'm guessing?"

"Happy as a cat with two bowls of cream. Have a great day, Mum. I'll catch you later." Dominic lifted a hand to Cameron, who nodded, then Dominic turned and went back to his car. Shortly afterward, she heard it pulling out of the car park.

The man of her dreams stood there, a small smile on his face, his eyes filled with hope. "Hello," he said.

"Hello." She closed the distance between them, her heart hammering. What on earth was he doing there? Had he come to try to persuade her to go with him to England again? Her pulse was racing so fast she felt a bit dizzy.

For a long moment, neither of them spoke. The high school had recently closed for summer, and a bunch of teenagers played around on the rocks leading across the river, laughing and splashing. Geese honked further up on the grass surrounding Kemp House, while a couple of bright blue pukeko birds nosed around in front of the restaurant. The sun was warm, and the river sparkled. Cameron's eyes were more blue than violet this morning, a beautiful color, like the sky above their heads.

Chapter Twenty-Seven

"What are you doing here?" Noelle asked eventually.

"I've come for you," Cameron said.

She swallowed hard. "Cam…"

Knowing she was going to tell him that she hadn't changed her mind about moving to England with him, he slid a hand to the back of her head, and bent and kissed her, long and lingering. She placed her hands on his chest but apparently couldn't bring herself to push him away, and closed her eyes. More relieved than he cared to admit, he wrapped her in his arms and enjoyed being close to her again, letting the warm sunshine banish all the dark dreams that had engulfed him since his accident.

When he eventually lifted his head, he touched a finger to her lips. "Don't say anything. I'm not here to ask you to come away with me."

She frowned. "Then…"

He slid a hand into the pocket of his jeans and extracted a gold coin. He held it for a moment, making a wish, and tossed it into the well.

Then he turned back to her and dropped to one knee.

"I'm here to beg your forgiveness," he said, looking up at her as she stared at him. "I've spoken to Marcus, and I've decided to take more of a back-seat role with the business. I'm giving up the diving and moving more into management, which I can do mostly online, from home. I'd like to move to New Zealand to oversee the waka project on the Hokianga. And, once again, I'd like to ask you to marry me. I love you, Noelle. I always have and I always will. Please forgive me for being such an idiot. Make me the happiest man in the world and say you'll be my wife."

Tears tumbled down her cheeks. "Oh God, yes, yes, yes!"

He stood, and she flung her arms around his neck, sobbing. "Shhh," he said softly, rubbing her back and kissing the top of her head. "It's supposed to be a happy thing!"

"I am happy. So happy. But oh Cam…" She moved back to look up at him, wiping her eyes. "Are you sure? I don't expect you to do this. Your business… I'm sure it needs you…"

"I have a great team, and everyone's on board to step up. We're making several promotions, and I'm confident it will go well." He let out a long sigh and took her hands in his. "I'm ready to move aside. To do something different. I'm not so attached to London that the thought of hot weather and a more relaxed lifestyle isn't appealing."

Noelle's eyes were filled with wonder. "What changed your mind?"

He'd been debating whether to tell her about the dive that had gone wrong. Marcus had nearly phoned her himself, but Cameron had yelled at him at the time that he didn't want her to know. Suddenly, though, he didn't want there to be secrets between them. "I had an accident, working on the San Jose."

Her eyes widened. "Oh no. What happened?"

"I'll tell you the details later. Basically I ran out of air and for a moment I thought I was going to die."

She pressed her fingers to her lips. "Oh, Cam…"

"It was scary, but I'm okay. The thing is, in those few seconds I knew immediately what an idiot I'd been. Nothing is more important to me than being with you."

"But your kids…"

"Yes, they are dear to me, but I'm not close to them the same way that you are to your children. I can fly back to see them once or twice a year, and I'm happy to pay for them to come for a visit—I'm sure they'd all love to see New Zealand."

She pressed her lips together, looking as if she couldn't believe it. "And your job… you're sure? You've spent so long building Subaqueous up…"

"I know we're not old, not even retirement age yet, but I'm ready to hand on the baton. I don't want to dive anymore." The accident had frightened him, although he wouldn't admit it to anyone. He didn't want to die when he had so much to live for. "I'll still play an active role, and I'll be talking to Marcus every day no doubt."

"I bet he was broken-hearted when you told him your plans."

He smiled. "He told me to 'go get the girl.'"

More tears glimmered on her lashes. "You really mean it? You really want to move here with me?"

"I do. I should have done it when we were twenty, and I'm sorry to have lost those years with you. But I know you were happy with Hugh, and he gave you your lovely children, so it was obviously meant to be. We have many, many years to look forward to together. And I'm determined to make the most of every one. Of every day. Every minute."

He pulled her into his arms. "I've asked Dominic if he would marry us at his church if you said yes. You can choose everything else—whether you want a big or small do, or just the two of us, I don't care. As long as you'll be my wife, I'll be happy."

He put a hand into the pocket of his jeans, pulled out a velvet box, and opened it. He studied her face, watching her reaction, and felt a rush of joy as her eyes lit with delight and her jaw dropped.

"I took the other ring back," he said huskily. "You were right, a ring should be about more than how big the diamond is. I had this one made specially." The dark stone in the center was circled by tiny red and blue stones. "The sapphires and rubies represent the English and New Zealand flag. And the black diamond represents New Zealand's All Blacks. It symbolizes the two of us coming together at last." It had cost around the same amount as the other ring, but he'd tell her that later.

"I love it." Tears trickled down her cheeks again as she took it out and slid it on. "It's beautiful, Cameron. Thank you."

He slipped his arms around her, closing his eyes against the glare of the sun on the river. "My wish came true," he murmured. "I'm so glad you said yes."

"I'm incredibly touched," she told him, resting her cheek on his chest, "by this grand gesture. I love you so much. I hope you know how difficult it was for me to walk away from you, both times."

"We'll say no more about it. From today, it's all about looking forward." He tucked a finger under her chin, lifted it, and kissed her. "I love you, Noelle Acton-Goldsmith. And I look forward to having a very long time to prove it to you."

She laughed and kissed him back, and then they stood there with arms wrapped around each other, in the light of the morning sun.

SERENITY WOODS

Newsletter

If you'd like to be informed when my next book is available, you can sign up for my mailing list on my website, http://www.serenitywoodsromance.com

I also send exclusive short stories and sometimes free books!

About the Author

Serenity Woods lives in the sub-tropical Northland of New Zealand with her wonderful husband and gorgeous teenage son. She writes hot and sultry contemporary romances. She would much rather immerse herself in reading or writing romance than do the dusting and ironing, which is why it's not a great idea to pop round if you have any allergies.

Website: http://www.serenitywoodsromance.com
Facebook: http://www.facebook.com/serenitywoodsromance
Twitter: https://twitter.com/Serenity_Woods

Made in the USA
Las Vegas, NV
30 April 2022